Hopper knew he was going to die.

He had only twelve aircraft left, and most of those had expended much of their ordnance. The Prl'lu had twice that many parent ships; he'd lost count of the smaller fighting craft and transports that were dropping down toward him. If they flew into that hornet's nest, they'd never get out again. But they had to.

He opened his mike. "Hopper to all ships. Forget the big ones up top. Forget the fighters. Go for the transports. They're the ones that'll give our people the most trouble."

An instant later he was among them.

WARRIOR'S WORLD

RICHARD S. McENROE

SF
ace books

A Division of Charter Communications Inc.
A GROSSET & DUNLAP COMPANY
51 Madison Avenue
New York, New York 10010

WARRIOR'S WORLD

An ACE Book

First Ace printing: October, 1981
Published Simultaneously in Canada

2 4 6 8 0 9 7 5 3 1
Manufactured in the United States of America

WARRIOR'S WORLD

WARRIOR'S WORLD

Prelude

The small blue world had suffered greatly in five short centuries, perhaps as much as at any time in its eons-long history. The slow corrosion and decay brought on by a dominant race reaching the limits of its resources and wisdom had been checked and wiped away by the cleansing disaster the few human survivors had called the Hammerfall—but that cleansing claimed a price. Gigatons of cometary matter disrupting the ecosystems of the Earth had wrought climatic changes that might never be reversed. The Earth was clean again—but it was not the world it had been.

Humanity might still have thrived. The scattered races of mankind might still have recovered and gone on, perhaps even to achieve the racial unity they had never attained in the past. They were a flexible species; they had a record of three and a half million years of adaptation and survival to prove it.

But they were never given the chance.

The first Prl'an stasis creche opened three hundred years after Hammerfall, somewhere in China, when the radiation from the brief but savage Russian/Chinese/Indian spasm of thermonuclear paranoia had subsided. Whatever else their unknown origin had shaped them for, the Prl'an had never been intended as warriors—but only the fierce could survive in the post-Hammerfall world. The Prl'an had not awakened empty-handed. They had supplies, and equipment, the tools and staples they would have needed to maintain and expand their foothold in whatever world they had been meant to awaken into. They fashioned arms from them, as though humans had gone to war riding farm tractors, brandishing jackhammers and surgeon's scalpels. It should never have worked. But there was nothing to oppose them.

In ten years the Prl'an had conquered China, what was left of it. Within a century, China had absorbed them as it had absorbed every other invader in its history. Another mystery, that this strange race could mix with mankind, and breed true—but undeniable fact. The Prl'an ways and traditions faded, even as they lost their true name, adopting instead the title of one of the Sinic races they ruled: Han. In place of their own heritage these new Han adopted an odd amalgamation of feudal Chinese practices and mannerisms, in bizarre contrast to the futuristic technology that supported their rule. No human scholar has ever been able to explain this puzzling self-aggrandizement.

Their control over the Chinese mainland secure, the Han turned their attention outward. Japan, the Korean peninsula and Southeast Asia fell quickly. The Han expanded swiftly through Siberia before encountering their first serious opposition in the rebuilding Russias. Had the shattered Soviets manifested their historic monolithicity, the Han threat might have ended there. But nuclear war and ethnic hostilities had lamed the Bear incurably. Europe fell as quickly.

The campaign for the Americas was a savage one.

Away from the coasts, the American continents had suffered in the main only from the secondary effects of Hammerfall. Some communications remained intact, some industry, some power, Central government had broken down quickly, but authority remained—at scattered military bases, at state and county seats with armories, but in most instances mainly in the hands of a few stubborn people who refused to surrender to the jungle. The suffering and loss of life matched that anywhere in the world in those first years—but the foundation upon which recovery could begin was just that little bit firmer.

When the first Han airships made their way south down the Pacific coast they encountered for the first time towns and cities, rather than scattered packs and tribes of barbaric nomads or crude dirt farmers. The humans had organization, this time, and discipline and communication—and weapons, the surviving armaments of a race that had honed killing itself to a fine art. There were one or two quick initial victories; then the Americans struck back with unprecedented savagery and skill. Many of the gleaming Han airships, that had razed the world with impunity, were torn shattered and burning from the sky.

In response to this defiance the Han stripped their other garrisons to the bone and hurled the accumulated fleets against the Americans. The battle raged for months, back and forth across the continent.

In the end, the Americans lost. Although the Han weapons were crude improvisations, they were crude improvisations based upon a technology orders of magnitude more sophisticated than that of the Americans. Although the Americans fought with intelligence and tenacity, they were fighting on their own territory—and there has never been a war fought with any weapon more sophisticated than a stone axe that has not done as much damage to the battlefield as to each combatant. Their cities were levelled, their industries destroyed, their populations driven into hiding.

But they were not broken. The Han withdrew,

as if destroying the symbols of human organization convinced them that they had destroyed the
intelligence that shaped those symbols. They
built great isolated cities, each a nest of savage,
hierarchical, infighting factions, linked by tenu-
ous airship routes and ruled in a pecking order
determined by the size and ruthlessness of their
respective airfleets. The humans they ignored,
save for the occasional self-indulgent "puni-
tive" raid. It was a safe course of action. In the
course of time they had inevitably learned that
human resistance had not been crushed in the
Americas, any more than it had been suppressed
anywhere else in the world. Indeed the Americans had rebuilt a society of remarkable novelty
and sophistication. But it was a weak society, in
the material and authoritarian terms that mattered to the Han. There was no way to form a
military structure that would topple the Han
cities within a "structure" of scattered, insular
communities and industries that had to be able
to pick up and run at the first approach of a Han
airship.

They tried, of course. American history of the
period reads like a catalogue of martyrs who
rallied one gang or another into an attack on the
Han. Each died, as martyrs will—and each got a
great many other people killed, as well. But they
kept coming. Martyrs are like that. Had the Han
realized that, they might have abandoned their
campaign of casual harassment in favor of a

serious effort at extermination. But by the time they learned that truth for themselves, it was too late.

Anthony Rogers may have been a wild card in history's hand—but surely no more so than the Han themselves. He had descended into a Pennsylvania mine shaft in 1929 A.D.—before Hammerfall, before Han—a young mining expert trying to put his own life together after the great disaster of his own time: a war meant, those who had not gone to fight all agreed, to end all wars. He never left that mine. An alien machine that had lain dormant for as long as the first Prl'an themselves stirred to life and trapped him within its own preservative stasis creche. When it next released him Rogers found himself in the world of the Han, of fugitive American gangs fighting to stay alive and marshal the strength to rid themselves of their oppressors.

Anthony Rogers had been a young officer of no special achievement in his first war; any number of intelligent, committed young men could and did perform his job. But in this new world he was indispensable. Rogers knew the value and the methods of unified action, a concept every American gang swore by and none had been able to make really work outside their own small groups.

Under Rogers the gangs finally gathered the strength to hurt the Han. City after city that had withstood the assault of individual gangs fell under the combined strength of two or three or a dozen. With Rogers' memories of large unit tactics, the very qualities of the new American culture that had hampered them in the past became their greatest strengths. They were so widely scattered that it was impossible for the Han to catch them in big, vulnerable concentrations. Each gang was so nearly self-sufficient that it was easy to collect effective forces near any objective. Within two years the last open Han city on the North American continent had been levelled, and Anthony Rogers found himself commanding the united military might of the gangs.

The next years reminded him more than anything else that his times were gone. The war against the Han had been a necessity for him: the gangs that had taken him in had needed his assistance. But for those gangs the war against the Han had been a crusade—and a war of extermination. Three hundred years of being hunted scarred too deeply for compassion. The American gangs took their war against the Han south and then east and west, across oceans and continents, seeking out the Han in their remaining holdings, in their very birthplace. They "liberated" the humans they encountered in the course of the campaign, naturally: the Asians, the Africans, the Europeans—at least insofar as they needed those survivors to carry weapons for them in their campaigns. Beyond that, the American influence beyond their own shores could best be described as benign neglect—as long as the rest of the world did nothing so foolish as obstruct American aims.

The butchering of the Han apalled Rogers—no less for his close contact with them during his long period of captivity among them in the course of the war of Liberation. But he made no protest; the sentiment of the gangs would not have permitted it. They demanded justice for three centuries of oppression that he had never experienced and could not ask to see put aside. And, to be honest, there was more to his silence than fear of negative reaction to outdated morality—it was also a convenient crypt in which to bury his own shame, born of the Han woman he had abandoned with child in his escape from the Han city. He thought she had died, at the time—another reason to doubt his motivation in pitying the Han. In the event, that pity had been worth little. By the time Rogers was effectively retired, shunted aside on the chain of command with the impressive if powerless title of Marshal of the Alliance, the Han had been decimated and more. His abandoned woman was only one death among many.

Except that the woman had not died—and neither had her son: Roger's son. Mordred. The Han held his human blood against him, for all that he was ultimately no more a bastard than any of them; he used their scorn as fuel to drive him toward an excellence beyond any achievement of theirs. They drove him from one hidden Han refuge to a lesser one all but forgotten in the depths of South America; as a result he lived when the refuge that exiled him was discovered and destroyed by the Americans, and went on to take control of the South American complex— from which he launched an assault meant to begin his revenge on his unacknowledged father.

Instead it signalled the beginning of a reign of terror unequalled since the days of Hammerfall. For all their sudden appearance among men, the Han did not lack mythology, and Mordred had come to believe that that mythology was based on fact. Much of that belief was self-delusion, of course. The Han had not been able to defeat humanity; yet it was obvious to any Han that mankind was a contemptible species of vermin. Therefore there had to be some power superior to humanity that was susceptible to Han control. Mordred thought he had found such a power, in the "warrior demons" of Han mythology. After years of searching, he discovered the lair of these "demons"—

He was wrong. The Prl'lu "warrior demons" were no tools to be used by the Han—they were a race at least as ancient as the Han's Prl'an ancestors—and their hereditary masters. Mordred found himself a scorned prisoner of the Prl'lu as they sought to break the back of the fledgling human civilization by melting the Antarctic ice-cap and drowning the shores of Earth.

The attempt failed, barely, as the Americans under Marshal Anthony Rogers managed to overrun the Prl'lu base at a heavy cost. The

course of the campaign provided at least one
wholly unexpected development: the rejuvena-
tion of the now-aged Rogers by the alien
device—now identified as a Prl'lu medical system—that had kept him alive for five hundred
years.

But even this setback failed to defeat Rogers'
Han sireling. Mordred had escaped the destruction of the Prl'lu holding him. He promptly fled
to one of the last Han redoubts on Earth, where
he used the fragments of Prl'lu military technology he had stolen to try and buy his way back
into power. Betrayed, he fled the city—just barely
in time to avoid the retaliatory assault following
the guerrilla attacks the Han had begun with the
Prl'lu weapons he had given them. Yet although
Mordred could flee the conséquences of his ac-
tions, he could not escape them, anymore than
could the world he acted against. The Han city
was destroyed, in part by the American attack—
and in part by the Prl'lu lunar base awakened by
the destruction of their Antarctic facility.

It might have comforted Mordred as he fled to
know that his failure had left Rogers with very
nearly as great a problem as his success might
have: the destruction of the Han redoubt had left
thousands of Han prisoners in the Americans'
hands, and a great many Americans wanted
those hands empty again—by whatever means
necessary. But Rogers was not willing to accept
cold butchery as a valid solution—not after so
many years of reconstruction and advancement;

especially not after so many years of guilt over his silence in the first massacres. But his reborn ethics clashed harshly with the rage and desire for revenge of all the gangs that had lost wives and husbands, sons and daughters to Han weapons.

If it hadn't been for the Prl'lu, the bickering American Alliance might have collapsed. But the attacks from the Prl'lu lunar base continued, directed now against humanity, rather than the Han. Mass-driver-launched projectiles rained down on North America; the gangs fled cities become deathtraps.

In a desperate bid for survival, Rogers took the Wilma Deering, the Alliance's sole functioning spaceship, with a hand-picked crew on a last-ditch voyage to Earth's satellite to subdue the alien threat. After a grim battle, Rogers triumphed—but not before the Prl'lu commander had issued the command to awaken every last Prl'lu detachment on Earth. It is here that we now leave the bare bones of simple history. . . .

CHAPTER
ONE

"Dammit, they're swinging back."

"Aknol," Holcomb said. "Get down under cover."

The hold of the clumsy transport was a cluttered maze of wiring and communications gear, hastily cobbled together into a working field outpost. The small, clear area of deck where Holcomb and the three techs worked, and the space little bigger where they lived with the flight crew between desperate engagements, were the only open areas in the ship.

The heavy forest around the transport concealed it well, as it concealed the vehicles, men and women of what had once been Badlands Air Base but was now nothing more than a band of weary guerrillas, short on supplies, short on transport, short of hope—short of everything except enemies who wanted them dead.

The sky above the forest was clear—save for the single Prl'lu scout ship swinging back towards the hidden human forces. The voice in Holcomb's headphones came from a single jump-belted spotter in a distant treetop, watching the Prl'lu hunter and reporting back through

the crudely-improvised directional radio trans-
mitters the humans had constructed. The ultronic communications that had given the
American rebels their great advantage in the first
War of Liberation were superior, for most purposes: they were much clearer, of indefinite
range, and untraceable. But by the same token,
they could not be shielded. An ultronic signal
was precipitated simultaneously, everywhere
within its range—and within that range it was a
dead giveaway that an operational target existed.
Radio signals could be tracked—but they had to
be detected first.

Holcomb could see the Prl'lu scout, now: a
tiny black mote in the distance. It grew as it
approached, but slowly; the scout ship was quar-
tering its flight path carefully in search of the
concealed guerillas. A second screen beside his
direct-vision plate glowed with a stylized map of
the terrain surrounding his forces. The Prl'lu
ship—a small red blip—closed in steadily, glid-
ing toward the clustered blue lights of Holcomb's forces.

He keyed in another channel. "They're coming in, Captain. You people ready?"

"We're ready, Major," Hopper's reply came
back to Holcomb from the grounded Mako
fighter three kilometers distant, as cool and dispassionate as it always was, as it had been even
on that chaotic day when the Prl'lu warcraft
came in out of nowhere and hit Badlands. There
had been a dozen of them, ten fighting ships

escorting two big troop transports. American planes had leaped desperately for the sky, only to be slashed at and struck down by weapons the humans had never even seen before. Ground positions were overrun by swarms of Prl'lu warriors, powerful and fast and savage beyond belief. The base would have been lost if not for Hopper. He had taken the surviving planes away from the base, climbing for altitude. Then he had brought them back, diving, with all the advantages of height and speed, hacking at the Prl'lu battle-craft in passing but concentrating their attack on the Prl'lu ground troops.

Hopper's cut-and-run tactics had paid off. The Prl'lu combat craft were there to support their ground operation; they were not free to break away and pursue the darting American craft—and they could not bring their superior firepower to bear on such quick, brief targets.

The Makos and the Falcons had broken the back of the Prl'lu infantry assault. The big Prl'lu gunships broke off and withdrew then, unable to deal effectively with the smaller, swarming ships that refused extended contact—and not needing to. The American aircraft had been chewed to ribbons in the first minutes of the attack. The fifteen ships Hopper had managed to rally were all that were left. The base itself was a burning, bloody shambles, still laced with gunfire where stunned, angry troops moved to eliminate scattered pockets of surviving Prl'lu. When the frantic pleas for aid began to come in from one gang and then another as Prl'lu strike forces began to overrun them, there had been nothing Will Holcomb could do. The inhuman fighters seemed to be everywhere at once. He had done the only thing he could. He had assembled what was left of the Badlands base and moved off into the field, away from the facility that now offered nothing but a target.

So now he sat in a crowded transport, watching the Prl'lu scout that could doom them all as it drew nearer and nearer. Now Hopper sat waiting in his Mako, with a dozen other ships around him, waiting to turn on their hunter. Three other pilots still waited with their ships as well, but they would not rise to fight. The planes were too badly damaged; their pilots knew themselves to be no longer warriors but ferrymen, hauling spare parts for the pursuits still able to give battle. They knew that when the need came, their ships would be sacrificed, stripped of weapons and armor and still-working systems to keep the other ships flying just that much longer. Then they would be just three more bodies among the two thousand scattered through the woods around them, their skills useless for want of the tools to apply them.

The Prl'lu scout ship was well inside the outer ring of Holcomb's observers now. His grounded planes were positioned to cut it off on any possible angle of retreat. He reached for his mike switch.

"All right—go!"

There were nearly two thousand men and women hidden in the forest beneath the Prl'lu scout. They were all that remained of the garrison and support elements of Badlands Air Base—and every one of them was armed, with the heaviest weapons they had been able to salvage from the base.

Small-arms rockets and heavy SHAPE missiles with their armor-piercing warheads turned the air around the Prl'lu scout ship to fire. It lurched and staggered under the multiple impacts as the thin blue cones of the dis batteries stole the air from beneath its wings, snatching the very atoms of the atmosphere away through myriad submicrosopic wormholes in the very fabric of space, to reappear at random beyond the influence of the beams.

If the Prl'lu ship had been moving at the full speed it was capable of, the attack would have failed. It would have been through the barrage and pulling away in less than a second. But to serve in its reconaissance role it had to fly slowly enough to see anything beneath it.

Even as the scout fell, even as it stabbed out with its auxilary repellor beams to steady itself against the earth beneath it, Hopper and his planes were leaping skyward: five of the powerful Mako fighters whose design had been largely borrowed from the Prl'lu ships captured during the Han Recurrence and seven of the lighter, nimbler, human-built Falcons. They surged up from the woods with all the power that was in them, standard *dis*-jet engines and secondary self-contained rocket boosters full open.

The Prl'lu ship was moving already, its *rep*-beams driving it upward as its own internal boosters sought to throw it clear of the *dis*-weapons shrouding it in vacuum. It was too late.

The Falcons were nowhere near as fast as the Prl'lu ship, or even the Makos they now out-stripped in their climb. They were lighter for their power, up to their performance limits: when they reached their peak speed the Makos would just keep accelerating—but up to that limit, the lighter ship would always have the edge.

The Prl'lu scout was boxed in perfectly. It couldn't even send out an alarm through the solid wall of ultronic and electronic jamming Holcomb's techs had thrown up. The Falcons swarmed all over it.

Dis and rockets washed over the scout's angular hull. Heavy SHAPE missiles struck full against its flanks, seeking to drive the armor-piercing payload of their shaped-charge warheads through the inertron armoring. None of the human weapons broke the Prl'lu ship's skin; the human weapons had been developed and adapted from years of battle with their slaughtered Han rulers—and the Han were a joke considered beside the Prl'lu. But even Prl'lu armor was not proof against concussion, against kinetic energy transmitted even more readily

through thick armor than thin air. The Prl'lu
scout was already hurting from the pummeling
Holcomb's ground batteries had given it; now
systems failed within its hull, structural members flexed and weakened. Eough of that pounding and even a Prl'lu ship could die.

So it attacked.

Even as it continued to build speed, the scout's
commander dropped flaps and kicked his rudder
hard over. The flaps added drag, and killed
much of the speed the scout had already gained,
but there was no chance of its stalling out with
the rep-rays bracing it away from the ground.
But the added degrees of flap also let the scout
turn more sharply than anything that big should
have been able to turn.

A darting Falcon found itself locked in the
sights of a Prl'lu fighting ship.

Fire erupted from the scout with astonishing
force. The pilot of the Falcon felt the brief sting of
the cardiogard disc taped over his heart as kar-
nak, the Prl'lu neural-disruption weapon, tried
to short his very autonomous nervous system.
Then the pain of the disc was lost as the first
Prl'lu shots detonated against his hull.

Even the armament of such a comparatively
light ship was astonishing in its variety. Missiles
struck and tore at the Falcon's inertron armor in
several different configurations; even solid slugs
slammed against the human ship's hull with
such rapidity that it was as though a bar of steel

was driven against its side. *Dis*, brighter and fiercer than the human variant, played over and around it as quick, savagely bright pulses of light like nothing the humans had stabbed into the hull, causing even the unyielding inertron plating to glow briefly red where they fell. Trapped in the Prl'lu *dis* beam, the Falcon could only keep on in its initial trajectory under the thrust of its internal rockets as it was slammed and battered by the incredible firepower being thrown against it.

Then the Makos hit the Prl'lu.

One Mako carried the firepower of three Falcons, condensed into one ship under one pilot's hands. Against one Prl'lu ship, a small one, that was just adequate.

The Makos broke off into two sections, three ships and two. Hopper took the larger element directly in against the scout. He wasn't looking for any extended engagement. He salvoed his full twelve SHAPE missiles into the Prl'lu ship, followed by the two Makos behind him. The Prl'lu scout staggered in flight; the exhaust of its internal boosters began to run smoky and uneven. But its weapons still tracked the helpless Falcon. The second flight of Makos closed, firing. The Prl'lu scout had taken all the punishment it could take. It yawed, tumbled—and the tangled wreckage of scout ship and Falcon plunged to the earth.

Even before the entwined ships struck ground

Holcomb was giving orders.

"All right, Major, get your people out of here—"

"What about Willits?"

"We're going after Willits." That was true, if Willits had been the flier of the downed Falcon. A boxy armored personnel carrier was already lifting out just over the treetops towards the crash site. Holcomb held little hope: any collision hard enough to distort inertron plating would have killed the pilot instantly through simple impact. They would look, of course; Holcomb had lost too many men to leave any more behind. But they would not find Willits alive.

"Company and section leaders, scatter. We'll reassemble at the next point on the RG list."

The woods around Holcomb's transport came to life. Transports, personnel carriers and light sleds went skimming away over the trees. Some of the smaller craft towed strings of personnel behind them on fine cable, their personal jump or rocket belts handling the lift requirement. They would meet again later, at a point determined by the randomly-generated list stored in each section's combat data system. Magnetic memory was a wonderful thing for troops on the run. If any given section of Holcomb's force was run to ground by the pursuing Prl'lu, the rendezvous points for the rest could be safeguarded forever at the flick of a switch. If only all their problems could be solved so easily. . . .

Holcomb felt the transport beneath him lift away from the ground and bank away from the abandoned positions. Speed was the key, now, the speed to get away from the Prl'lu forces sure to come looking for their missing scout. After the disaster at Badlands and the chase of the past weeks Holcomb had no illusions left about the outcome of any pitched battle between his forces and their Prl'lu pursuers. No, they would limit themselves to their present tactics, for as long as they could—hit and run and run again; stay alive, keep fighting, because when they were gone, Holcomb didn't know if there would be anyone else left to take up the job. . . .

The spikeslinger broke out of the brittlegrass in a rush of muscle and territorial outrage as the Prl'an workers scattered in panic. Jak't'rin ran forward. Alone, even one such as he was no match for the enormous beast, but the other sentinels would not reach the scene from their own posts in time to prevent carnage among the workers. The Prl'an were in his charge and he was of the Blood; he could not desert them.

The ground shook as the spikeslinger planted its elephantine forelegs. The momentum of its full six tons snapped its barbed tail forward over its arched back. The older spikes at its bulging tip—the longer, heavier ones no longer firmly rooted—were shaken loose and hurled forward like so many meter-long javelins.

With all his speed Jak't'rin barely had time to raise the hide-and-wicker buckler. One spike pierced it cleanly, yanking it from his grasp. Another dropped toward him; without thinking, he struck at it with the slender javelin he held in his other hand. The shaft of the javelin flexed alarmingly, but the spike was turned.

Without thinking, Jak't'rin reversed the weapon and hurled it against his attacker. It struck powerfully; Jak't'rin's arm, longer than a man's and more prominently jointed, was a naturally efficient lever.

The spikeslinger bellowed and shook its barrel-sized head; the javelin was dislodged and fell from its neck. The bright patch of scarlet blood looked very small against the mottled hide.

The slinger lurched into motion again. No beast its size could build up to a charge with any great rapidity—but no beast its size was going to be halted easily, either.

Jak't'rin drew one of his short, heavy fighting spears from the quiver at his back and fitted it to the throwing-stick he readied in his other hand.

He took his stance, waiting for the spikeslinger to come within range, committed to its charge. The slinger roared and its challenge reverberated within Jak't'rin's chest, like an angry fist pounding on his heart. A lesser being would have fled: the Prl'an workers had already abandoned the field. Jak't'rin stood his ground. His dark, deeply set eyes registered no feeling as the slinger's roar thundered through him, but his grip tightened on the armed throwing-stick he drew

back and readied; the buckler on his warding
arm was extended just the least big further in
balance. Power flooded him as he prepared to
fight; strength born of glandular action and
awareness of purpose. His very skin tingled with
it, from clenched weapon hand to the crest of
stiff black hair rising from his brow. He was of
the Blood and he would fight for those in his
charge. He would defend those few meters of
bare earth upon which he stood as if they were
Hrak'un'Mrak, the Place of Awakening, itself. He
could do nothing else.

He was Prl'lu.

The spikeslinger pounded into range. Jak't'-
rin's arm snapped down and the spear flew fair,
to bury itself deeply at the base of the slinger's
neck. Even as it roared again, this time almost
shrilly, in pain, Jak't'rin leaped forward, striking
again with his throwing-stick. The heavy metal
blades set around its end made it a formidable
mace.

He struck the slinger full in the face, aiming for
an eye, a difficult target in its deep socket of
heavy bone. He had no time to see if his blow had
struck home as he twisted out of the spikeslinger's path—and the barbed tail caught him solidly
in the back.

The blow would have killed a lesser
creature—but Prl'lu were remarkably hard to
kill. Leathery skin that would have turned a
knife blade withstood the jabbing spikes well
enough to safeguard internal organs no less vul-

nerable than any; ribs joined together with more than the human amount of cartilage flexed under the impact, but did not break. Jak't'rin was thrown heavily to the ground, the endentate ridges that served him in place of fragile teeth clashing violently as he landed—and he was up again, discarding his throwing-stick/mace for another short spear. The shallow puncture wounds where the slinger's tail had gouged him were already scabbing over. He levelled the spear in the high-ready stance, and braced for the slinger's next attack.

The slinger had plunged a dozen meters past him, borne on by its own weight, before it could slow and turn. The deadly tail slashed the air behind it as it whirled, warding against any foes behind it. Jak't'rin thought the beast an uncommonly skilled fighter for a plant eater.

Blood seeped thickly from torn flesh above the spikeslinger's left eye. He had missed the organ itself, but from the way the slinger carried its head, Jak't'rin could tell that the cut was interfering with its sight.

The beast located its tormentor again and stumbled powerfully into motion. It bore down on him with increasing swiftness as he settled more firmly into his stance and readied his spear—

—the slinger shrieked in outrage and crashed onto its side as it tried to turn too quickly. The hafts of half a dozen javelins rose from its flank. Beyond it, six Prl'lu warriors hurled a volley of fighting spears that struck deeply into its soft underbelly.

The slinger was possessed of a terrible vitality. Even as another flight of spears tore at it, it was lurching to its feet and staggering off back into the deep grass. Jak't'rin looked after it as it disappeared from view.

They had wounded the beast badly, he knew. Yet it might be days before it finally died. That could not be allowed; a party would have to follow it into the bush and finish the killing. The animal had merely been defending its territory; it did not deserve to suffer for that.

But they would not set out after it today. Already the sun was beginning to sink below the horizon, and even through the perpetually hazy sky the bright blue point of the evening star could be seen rising higher overhead.

As he returned his spear to his quiver and retrieved his throwing-stick, Jak't'rin thought on that tiny pinpoint of light and those of the Blood the histories said could be found there. He wondered if they yet slept, or if one not unlike him might perhaps be looking to the end of his own duties with the satisfaction of a responsibility well born. . . .

The world spun around Shak't'kan as he stood in the center of the observation chamber, adjusting the enormous hologram around him to focus on the trapped humans.

They were well positioned, for what that mattered. Considering their crude armament and comparative lack of fighting skill, Shak't'kan doubted they could do any better. These mysterious natives were no fighters; it was almost as if some fluke of nature had duped Prl'an into believing they were Prl'lu—although these beings were unquestionably better combat material than the degenerate Han mongrels the Blood had so quickly disciplined upon Awakening. This group he studied now might be trapped, but there were others that were proving no easy prey at all.

Shak't'kan turned. The landscape continued unbroken behind him, with no sign of walls or doorway. It was as if the thin metal ramp upon which he stood hung suspended in space, free of all support. Had he cared to order it, the landscape would have rushed past beneath and around him, covering miles in seconds, to look down on the scene where his last scout ship had been lost. He had learned better than to rush forces into the area; perhaps these humans were no match for the Prl'lu in battle but their mobility was excellent and their field tactical systems surprisingly sophisticated. They would be long gone and impossible to find save by the physical searches already being carried out.

Shak't'kan didn't smile. His face could not shape such an expression. His lips lacked the flexibility required; where brow and nose would have been on a human face he possessed heavy, immobile ridges of sharp bone, that gave excellent protection to eyes and vulnerable nasal cavities but displayed little emotion. Yet if he could have smiled, he would have.

The human commander was using his forces well, better than had been expected. He was compensating for his inescapable weakness with speed and mobility, the way Shak't'kan would have in the same circumstances. But there was one mistake the human commander could not help but make—and that was how Shak't'kan would win. *If* the humans would act as he thought they must, and there was one sure way to check that. He touched a key on the small console before him.

"Bring me the prisoner," he said.

He would not fear, Mordred told himself with that part of his mind that was still free to feel so. But so great a part of him was locked into the ancient terror. . . .

He had never before felt such fear, not in all the years of scorn and hatred he had endured among the fallen Han who had despised him for his human ancestry; not in the campaigns against the Americans; not even in his first time of captivity among the Prl'lu themselves. He had not known them, then. The Prl'lu had merely been a legend come real, the demon warriors he hoped to manipulate in the extermination of the Americans.

How quickly that had gone wrong. The Prl'lu had accepted Mordred's 'rule,' just long enough to activate their Antarctic base, just long enough to learn something of the strange world into which they had awoken. Then they had overpowered their Han summoners with horrible ease, and gone on to launch an assault that threatened half the planet in their attempt to bring the insurgent race of man under Prl'lu control. They had failed, and Mordred had escaped, solely through bad luck and the unexpectedly superior leadership of Marshal Anthony Rogers, Mordred's unacknowledged human father.

Mordred learned from his errors. When next he set out to confront his father's people, he gave a wide berth to the remaining caches of Prl'lu, still preserved in their unbreachable stasis fields, that had been located—and when he fled the Han who betrayed him at the height of an American attack, he had stumbled straight into and roused Shak't'kan's undiscovered facility.

The efficiency with which the Prl'lu set out to subjugate mankind astonished him. The humans had already been driven from their cities by the time Mordred was taken prisoner, their communities shattered by mass-projector-driven projectiles from the Moon. Then the hunt began, the tracking-down of the scattered American gangs. Shak't'kan had needed Mordred then, for the knowledge of men that the Han bastard had gained while the Prl'lu commander slept in timeless stasis. Mordred had cooperated, in spite of his growing conviction that the humans might be a lesser danger to his surviving people than the Prl'lu. He cooperated because he had lied, once—and the grim-faced Prl'lu interrogators and their sterile, oh-so-efficient machines had nearly killed him.

Mordred knew his information would only buy him limited time. The Prl'lu had nothing but contempt for the Han, who they regarded as re- bellious inferiors. When the last of the humans were subjugated—or when Shak't'kan decided Mordred knew nothing more of use—his luck would run out unless he could compose a plan of action. That would not be easy. When your enemy has the advantage of you in numbers, ability, resources and probably intelligence, your options are somewhat restricted. . . .

The Prl'lu escorting him down the corridor paid Mordred little direct attention. That was characteristic of these grim creatures; the Prl'lu knew that Mordred was no threat to him and so could not be troubled to observe him more closely than necessary to keep him moving in the right direction. That could be a weakness, Mordred knew—if he had been able to do any- thing with it. But against a being that stood a full foot-and-a-half taller than himself, whose empty hands looked like knobbed bludgeons in and of themselves—Mordred walked along.

The world was spinning around him as he entered Shak't'kan's observation chamber. Sky and soil rushed past the slender pylon at an incredible rate. Mordred fought off a stab of ver- tigo as the horizon canted sharply around him and a great pillar of smoke came into view beyond the pylon.

Shak't'kan turned briefly to acknowledge Mordred's arrival, then resumed his study of the scene before him. It was forest, laced through with smoke and fire. Black Prl'lu ships circled and dove above the conflagration, as pale sweeps of *dis* and bright-bursting missiles tore at the air around them.

"Versatile creatures," Shak't'kan said. "This was no fighting force. They moved with young, and non-military stores, and members who cannot or will not fight. Yet they resist well, considering."

"But surely not successfully."

"Quite successfully—as long as that suits my purposes." Shak't'kan turned. "You will tell me if it does."

"I have little choice," Mordred said.

"And less manners. You should at least finally have learned your place by now."

Mordred paused, remembering the bright machines. "That . . . has been made clear to me. How may I serve you?"

"With an 'educated' opinion. These humans have defeated you often enough for you to have learned something of their ways. So tell me, from any such knowledge you may possess—will one band of humans put itself at risk for another?"

"That was how they defeated us."

"No. Your degenerate ancestors defeated themselves when they abandoned their respon-

sibilities and left us to sleep while they played
with power above their station. That is perhaps
how the humans outfought you, but I must
know if they will do so consistently."

"Humans are not consistent, except in their
perversity. I cannot say if one gang will imperil
itself for another at this point. You've hurt them
badly, and I suspect that each gang will be concerned mostly for its own safety now."

"Each gang. Gangs are these mixed parties,
such as the one before you now?"

"That is correct."

"Then what about a unit composed solely of
warriors?"

"That would be different. They would see it as
their responsibility to protect a gang at risk, yes.
Under a strong leader, they might even put that
goal above their own survival."

"Of course. How else?"

"Easily else," Mordred said. "These humans
are not—" he shied away from the word 'fana-
tics' "—so singularly dedicated to one purpose
as are the Blood. Their own welfare concerns
them, to a great extent, above all else."

"And that is why they lose. Yet under a strong
leader, they might behave decently?"

Decently by the standards of the Blood,
Mordred thought, decently enough to die blood-
ily and uselessly—

"Yes."

Shak't'kan turned to look back at the screen.
"Good."

Rogers stared up at the pale blue planet, watching his world end.

Even the sophisticated systems of the Prl'lu observation chamber could not pick up sufficient detail to let him follow the scattered hopeless battles going on beneath him. Anthony Rogers had to rely on the communications set-up aboard the battered *Wilma Deering* for that. He spent long hours there, while the surviving crew made a point of ignoring his grim vigil.

Europe was lost. The last fragmented messages had spoken of scattered strong-points in the Alps—but that was a week ago. From the British Isles to western Russia, there was nothing to hear but the harsh, glottal speech of the Prl'lu conquerors.

There was still communication out of Asia and Africa, and to some extent South America. The land itself resisted the invaders there: there were not enough Prl'lu to garrison those enormous continents effectively. But the ones there were were enough to keep the surviving free populations in constant retreat. When centers of resistance did coalesce, the Prl'lu fell upon them savagely—and they hadn't lost yet.

Rogers was beginning to doubt they would. Only Australia held out so far. No Prl'lu had yet awakened within their borders, and the mixed Australo-Asiatic population was guarding its territory grimly. Prl'lu exploratory raids were driven back in bitter fighting—but the Australians could not launch a sustained attack across thousands of miles of ocean in defense of the rest of the world, not by themselves, and there was no one to help them.

The captured Prl'lu base at Earth's south pole was silent. Rogers was thankful that at least the Prl'lu had not retaken that formidable outpost. He had no way of knowing that the human garrison had prevented that only by reactivating the base's stasis field, trapping defender and attacker alike in a layer of frozen time.

Human voices still reached the Moon from North America. A scattered collection of gangs under Boss Loup-main fought a running battle back and forth across the icy fringes of the Arctic Circle. The gangs of the Florida peninsula were rooted in deeply amid the Everglades, green and tangled as ever five centuries after Hammerfall. Several hundred survivors of the Southwestern SubCouncil and several thousand members of the Central American gangs clung to freedom in the mountains of northern Mexico and the Baja Islands. The remaining free gangs of the North American Alliance—there weren't many— sought safety with one or the other enclave, and several units of the shattered federal forces still fought a fluid guerrilla campaign.

But they couldn't win like that, Rogers knew. Not against the Prl'lu. So far the enigmatic aliens had elected to fight the battle for Earth with a level of armament proportionate to their enemies'—their aircraft were more heavily armed and faster, their ground units devastating, their tactics dismayingly effective—but those were differences of degree, not kind. Rogers was certain that a race that could build the facility he stood in, that had launched hundred-ton projectiles against the Earth with enough force to shatter cities, could employ weaponry as far beyond what humanity possessed as those were beyond the bolt-action rifles and horse-drawn field pieces of Roger's first life in the twentieth century. Evidently the Prl'lu wanted to take the Earth, not destroy it.

And Rogers could not stop them. He was the Marshal of the Alliance's armed forces, the one man with any record of success against the Prl'lu, and he was trapped a quarter of a million miles away from the battle, watching his forces being broken up and destroyed piecemeal.

The *Deering* could have returned him to Earth, where he could have been helpless much closer to home. The Prl'lu had seemed to erupt everywhere, at once. Even Anthony Rogers could only be in one place at a time. The *Wilma Deering* herself was no match for the Prl'lu aircraft that ruled Earth's sky, even before the pounding she had taken in the attack on the Prl'lu lunar base her crew now occupied. Rogers stood in a chamber beneath the surface of the Moon, with a half-wrecked ship and a score of men and women at his command, and considered the loss of all he had fought for.

Angrily, he slapped a switch on the jury-rigged panel before him, a panel that replaced the molten slag of the original Prl'lu unit, destroyed by the base's commander. If he could have slammed the sliding hatch at the inboard end of the observer's pylon, he would have.

The machinery was maddening.

Ruth Harris leaned over the Prl'lu console, stylus in hand, meticulously transcribing the angular alien script into what she hoped was its correct English equivalent. There was no way she could be certain she was right. Some of the Prl'lu systems were comprehensible, based on her experience in the Antarctic complex. Some of their functions were deducible, based on nerve-wracking experimentation. But too much of it wasn't, and they weren't making nearly enough progress as they had to.

It wasn't a fair situation. In three years, with a trained scientific staff, Ruth Harris had only begun to scratch the surface of the massive Prl'lu complex at Earth's South Pole. Now, with only a handful of technicians operating outside their fields, she was trying to analyze an entire new facility, against a deadline that might already have passed. She had to assume that she was the only trained person left with an opportunity to study their attackers and the freedom to act on whatever knowledge she could gain. Back on Earth men and women she had known were fighting and losing against the demon warriors; the Prl'lu base was the one wild card they held that might still pay off. So Ruth Harris didn't ask for a fair situation—she played to win with the one she had.

The door slid open behind her and Rogers entered the room. It was a measure of how desperately tired Ruth Harris was that she took pleasure from seeing him, that she felt only an irrational guilt at not having solved all his problems personally. It *was* irrational to feel that way, she knew that—she also knew that she was a long way from adjusting to a girlish crush on an elderly man abruptly transformed into a returned love from a rejuvenated hero of the Alliance. Dammit, one Prl'lu machine had given her that; why couldn't these let her save a world for him?

"How's it going, Ruth?" Rogers asked.

"Not too badly," she answered. "I haven't blown the base up yet, or vented our atmosphere into space, and no one's turned blue and dropped dead whenever I pushed a button. Beyond that, I'd have to say progress has been limited, to put it mildly."

"Then you're doing better than the rest of the human race put together. What *have* you learned?"

"Learned? Nothing. Guessed, inferred, supposed, hypothesized, imagined—a lot. Too much; nothing consistent. It may be petty of me, but I can't help wishing these people had just left a few dozen technical manuals laying around when we wiped them out."

"In English, of course."

"Of course. With lots of simple pictures. But they didn't." Her brief smile faded, and Rogers could see the fresh lines that weariness and worry had drawn at the corners of her mouth and eyes. "So, we push buttons, and pull levers, and hope nothing kills us before we figure out what it does."

"And have you figured out what this does?"

She gestured at the room around them. "This? Not hardly, Marshal Rogers sir. What does it look like to you?"

Rogers looked around. "Isn't that the bell of a dis projector?"

"Uh-huh."

"Aimed at the floor?"

"Well, at the podium beneath it, but the question's the same."

"That's one large emissions bell," Rogers said. He was stating the obvious. The bell was a good three meters across, and oblong; if he hadn't recognized the dis-resistant alloy lining it, he would never have guessed at its function. "What could it be for?"

"There's only one way to tell," Ruth said.

Rogers shook his head. "I'm not sure I can allow that, Ruth. We have enough problems without vaporizing the bottom half of the base."

"I don't think that's all that likely," she answered. "There's no reason to assume that the Prl'lu would set up a weapon just to destroy their own facility."

"Wouldn't they? Rather than let it fall?"

"It did fall, Tony. And there are easier ways to wipe out a base like this than disintegrating it a few square meters at a time."

"True."

"Besides, I'm not all that sure that this *is* just a *dis* beam. The beam-generation unit is only a part of the system."

"And the rest?"

Ruth sighed. "Now you're getting fussy again." She pointed at the console before her. "This is *some* kind of operator-input system; this panel here is some sort of direct operations control—power on/off, intensity modulation, we know that much from the other systems we studied. Thank God the Prl'lu are a very methodical people: they really made a habit of systems standardization. But *this,* over here—" she indicated another panel of instruments "—*this* is a problem." She threw a switch on the first panel and the boards lit up. A vertical column of angular Prl'lu script tumbled down one side of the screen above the console, followed by another beside it. "Maybe you can tell me what those are."

"Choices, of some kind."

"I know that; I even know how to indicate my choice." She touched a button and one after the other, the listings on the screen blazed more brightly than the others, each in its rapid turn. She took her finger off the button and one selection remained highlighted. "But what are we selecting for? Functions? Extensions? Flavors? I've no idea which."

"And there's only one way to tell, isn't there?"

"I'm afraid so, Tony. So, if you don't mind leaving the room—"

"You're not going to stay here either," Rogers said.

"Somebody has to push the 'on' button."

"That somebody doesn't have to be you, Ruth."

"That somebody may as well be me. We're in the middle of the base, Tony, and the Prl'lu were very careful systems engineers. Even if this thing is capable of doing something catastrophic, it won't do it just because we've turned the power on."

"So you'll pick a setting at random, push the button and see what happens?"

"It's how we've been working since we took this place. We don't stand to gain anything by stopping now."

Rogers sighed unhappily. "All right. Go ahead, then."

"Just as soon as you leave the room, Tony."

"I thought you said there wasn't any chance of anything catastrophic happening."

"A safe risk for a frustrated scientist isn't a safe risk for the remaining government of the Alliance."

"Some government. Push the button, Ruth."

"Why are you being so stubborn about this, Tony?"

"Selfishness, I guess."

"What?"

"So far I've managed to lose a nation, a continent, and a planet," Rogers said, ignoring Ruth's interrupting denial, "not to mention a few odd centuries of history. If I have to run the risk of losing a woman who happens to be one of my last reasons for hanging around, I'd just as soon not be around to be aware of it. Peculiar, but there it is."

"Well, I guess so," Ruth said, and smiled. "And I suppose it should be rather flattering, in its guilt-ridden way." She shrugged. "All right. Let's give it a try." She turned back to the selection dial, then shook her head. "Forget it. One's as good as the next."

She turned back to the operator input panel. She touched a switch and the emissions bell of the great *dis* unit across the room began to glow, outlined in pale blue radiance. She reached for another, larger button, one of a pair set one above the other. She put three fingers to the button and pressed, hard, to overcome springs geared to Prl'lu strength.

The *dis* beam stabbed down at the podium beneath it—and as they watched, the door appeared. . . .

Rogers cursed and grabbed for the pistol he wasn't wearing.

The Prl'lu warrior on the other side of the doorway was not so unprepared. It snapped its head around from the console it had been studying and in almost the same instant was up from its chair and lunging forward, drawing the weapon it wore holstered at its hip—and the glowing doorway vanished as Ruth Harris slammed a fist down on the lower button of the pair.

The long-fingered Prl'lu hand skittered across the floor and struck wetly against her foot. Ruth yelped in disgust and kicked it away; it lay palm up on the floor, in a thick film of rich inhuman blood.

Rogers straightened, slowly, from his instinctive fighting crouch. The two of them looked down at the severed hand.

"I . . . don't think we want to try that selection again, doctor."

"No, probably not. . . ."

CHAPTER TWO

They stood well apart, in a broad semicircle just within the treeline. They came armed for war and prepared for battle, with bucklers raised and spears fitted to throwers.

Jak't'rin faced them, his own shield readied, his own weapon in his hand. Behind him the warriors who followed him stood in open formation in three loose ranks, too widely spaced for an effective massed volley against them. They also stood with spears fitted and ready, but they were not here for Jak't'rin's protection. If violence erupted their first volley would be directed at the intruding Prl'lu facing them and the others hidden in the trees. Jak't'rin would be doomed, standing forward and exposed as he did; there would be no way for him to escape.

But he did not mean to escape. If it came to battle that day, his one ambition would be to kill the warrior standing before him; if he could do that, his death would be well rewarded.

Chen't'kin was the fighting-chief of the Outer Lines, leader of the Blood that protected the Prl'an work units furthest away from Hrak'un'Mrak, out where the spikeslingers and even worse predators were as thick as the brittlegrass that concealed them, where the forest itself resisted their attempts to expand.

"I say it is time they awake," he said, abandoning honorifics, ignoring the politeness one fighting-chief should have accorded another.

"You have said as much twice before," Jak't'rin answered. The Outer Lines warrior overstood him by half a hand's breadth; his fighting stick was scarred and his buckler discolored by many brighter patches of overweaving where old damage had been repaired. But buckler and stick and the arms that wielded them were still as strong as any. "And twice I have argued against you."

"No," Chen't'kin said. "Once I counseled such, and was ignored. Once I asked as much, and was refused. Now I will demand it."

"And I will speak you as I spoke you before. It is not for us to force the Shapers from their slumber. It is folly to suggest it, dangerous arrogance. They ruled here, as is right, not us. It is for the Blood only to obey their will."

"A will they do not express," Chen't'kin said. "A will they cannot express while they sleep!"

"They have expressed it. We have their words from our fathers, and their fathers before them for five names' time. We must guard the Prl'an, and see them prosper, and tend the Place of Awakening until the Shapers arise to lead us to our glory. What other will can they express now?"

"We have obeyed their words. The Prl'an do prosper. We have increased their numbers and the land they tend fivefold and more."

"Then you should be content to have served so truly," Jak't'rin said.

"But we may yet serve them better, warrior! Let us rouse them, and show them how well they are served. Can they then deny that it is time to take up their place among us again, and lead us into triumph over all this world? Can they?"

As strongly as he had the first two times they had contested, Jak't'rin felt the seductive power of Chen't'kin's plea. They were fighting-chiefs; they had been privileged to make the pilgrimage to Hrak'un'Mrak itself and to be granted entrance by the great iron sentinels. Jak't'rin had seen the majesty of the future that awaited them, the great tools of unguessable purpose and inarguable power, that would one day be given over to the Blood—that might be given over to *him*, if he might prove worthy. . . .

No.

What he imagined was madness, was *wrong*, for all that it drew him like a bright flame. Was he a Shaper, then, to twist destiny, to abandon the service of generations for his own ambitions? He could not; he was of the Blood, that and no more, and it was all he would ever be.

It was all he would ever need.

"The Shapers will sleep," he said to the warrior who faced him. "While I or any of my line live the Blood will wait, and serve."

"Then you must not live."

"It comes down to that," Jak't'rin agreed. "*Shak'si arek.*" *Divine honor to the Shapers.*

"*Ahgn'ki Prl'lu!*" Chen't'kin cried: *Blood of the Blood*, the old battle cry.

And he struck.

Jak't'rin stepped back and to the side as Chen't'kin lunged forward, his fighting stick cutting down through the space he had just abandoned. Jak't'rin returned the blow, a sidewise, slashing attack deflected by Chen't'kin's buckler, though fresh wounds were torn in its thick weaving. Chen't'kin kicked out and Jak't'rin retreated again, out of range, as his opponent landed cleanly, braced to counter any riposte.

They stood for an instant, briefly disengaged, as the ranks of warriors around them tensed and prepared to loose their javelins at the first interference by either side. Then Chen't'kin rushed again, in a wheeling circular attack, striking out with fighting stick and buckler's rim and low, strong kicks meant to bruise and weaken Jak't'rin's legs.

Jak't'rin gave ground steadily, deflecting stick blows with his buckler, not trying to stop them directly and risk damage to his shield, jumping forward to jam Chen't'kin's kicks and rob them of their power, then leaping back as stick and buckler came around again.

Chen't'kin broke off his attack; not even a Prl'lu could maintain that savage pace indefinitely. Jak't'rin was not deceived; he knew his enemy was far yet from the limits of his strength.

But he thought he had his measure now.

He settled into a deep fighting stance, faking a slight awkwardness as though Chen't'kin's kicks had accomplished at least part of their purpose. He brought his buckler in close, tight to his body, defensively—but also obscuring Chen't'kin's view of his grip on his fighting stick, so that the Outer Lines fighting-chief did not see how he reversed the weapon and laid its shaft up along his forearm, so that only six inches of its metal-shod end extended past his hand. Chen't'kin raised his weapon and extended his buckler, stepping forward—

Jak't'rin sprang. Chen't'kin tried to bring his buckler into line but Jak't'rin's own shield was already there, blocking it, rising into his face. Chen't'kin chopped at him but Jak't'rin was already within the fighting stick's arc. The shaft of the weapon bounced off his shoulder as Jak't'rin drove the haft of his own weapon forward into Chen't'kin's side. The Outer Lines warrior cried out in sudden pain and staggered back, doubled over the blow, and Jak't'rin followed. He reversed his weapon again and slashed down, ripping through Chen't'kin's buckler. He kicked, and the warrior lurched backward and fell, rolling clumsily upright again—

—and the ruined buckler flew aside in a tangle of wicker as Chen't'kin released it and sped the short spear over his shoulder from its quiver and across the scant feet separating them. It pierced Jak't'rin's buckler and drove on to put point to his shoulder, ripping a deep gash in the rope-like muscles there. The spear pulled loose as he discarded his buckler and reached for one of his own spears, shifting his fighting stick to his buckler-hand.

The two fighters paused again. Chen't'kin stood oddly stooped, favoring his injured side. Jak't'rin was forced to hold his fighting stick higher than he liked, to keep the rich blood welling slowly from his shoulder from running down his arm and weakening his grip. Neither chief spoke, though others would talk of this fight for years to come. Each warrior had thought only for his opponent.

Chen't'kin advanced again, and this time Jak't'rin retreated not from choice but from necessity. Chen't'kin's kicks had lost none of their power, his stick-blows none of their accuracy—and no matter how he whirled and weaved and dodged, the point of his opponent's spear seemed fixed in the air before him, always seeking Jak't'rin, always inhibiting his counter-attack.

Try as he would to keep the stick high, the blood from his wound was working its way down his arm as blocked and parried Chen't'kin's attacks. He felt the first warm trickle over his wrist and knew that soon he would be unable to keep a strong grip on his fighting stick. Then, half-disarmed, he would no longer be able to hold off Chen't'kin, and he would die, and the Outer Lines fighting-chief would journey to Hrak'un'Mrak and he would seek to awaken the Shapers and Jak't'rin would have failed—

He bellowed in blind, angry denial, cast his fighting stick aside, and threw himself into Chen't'kin's attack. The spearpoint sought him and tore his shoulder again, but he twisted and pulled free, ignoring the pain. He hooked his arm over Chen't'kin's as the spearpoint slid past his neck, using his weight and the leverage of the pinned weapon to lock them together and his own spear, close-gripped, plunged into Chen't'kin's side again and again, deeply, stabbing and stabbing. Chen't'kin struck him savagely upon the back with his fighting stick and the breath was driven from Jak't'rin's lungs. He went to his knees but he didn't let go, and he drove his spear up into his enemy over and over and over—

He was laying face down in the moist earth, his chest sticky and clotted with his own blood. With an effort, he made himself let go of the crusted spear still gripped in his good hand, and forced himself slowly up to his knees.

Chen't'kin lay awkwardly, his legs doubled up beneath him. Jak't'rin could remember pulling the Outer Lines warrior down as he sagged, but nothing further. He didn't remember seeing him die.

He looked up, and saw the line of warriors facing him from the trees. Somehow, he got to his feet. Somehow, he mastered the swaying, conquered the dizziness that threatened to pull him down again. Somehow, he reached up over his shoulder, and took another spear in his good hand, and faced them, waiting.

The Outer Lines warriors watched him, for a moment that seemed to go on forever—and then they turned and melted away into the trees again.

Then Jak't'rin let himself fall again, as his warriors clustered around and lifted him to their shoulders. As they carried him onto the path back to the village, he dreamed of words of praise and approval spoken in Shapers' voices, and of bright, gleaming machines listening to his orders. . . .

She has turned the very world against us, Talinai thought in horror. Great spikes of stone were heaving themselves up from the once-featureless plain, tearing through black soil and thick moss and scattering their small party.

Sirunir died there and then, caught by a soaring granite spear and thrown high into the air, to land heavily and lie unmoving where he fell. Aslinon and Pehr were lost to sight in a shower of torn soil, and Couilin screamed, inaudibly amid the greater cries of the violated earth, and fled, abandoning his weapons and his friends.

Talinai threw herself down, curled around the shaft of her javelin, knowing there was no way to hide from this new attack, surrendering her life to chance. She was thrown violently to one side as a new column of rock burst skyward, and she tumbled away in a shower of dirt and stones. The noise was incredible, almost beyond direct perception; it seemed to born as much within her body as in the shattered land around her.

Then suddenly there was silence, almost unrecognized in its unfamiliarity. Talinai risked standing, straightening gracefully to her feet, leaning on her javelin.

Of their party there remained three: herself, Dunlimin, and Pehr, who forced his way stiffly from beneath a pile of rubble. *All that Blood weaponry of his finally did him some good*, she thought, *though he has yet to strike an effective blow against the Monster with it.*

But then none of them had, so far. They stood in the midst of the ravaged plain, three living out of six, and those six all that remained of a hundred and more, and they had never seen their enemy, or managed to raise a hand against her.

Dunlimin straightened the hem of her robe, trying to brush away some of the grime of their travels.

"Well, brave warriors, once again your great skill at arms have saved us from disaster," she said sarcastically. "While your noble Shaper's will obviously served us so successfully," Talinai answered. She and Dunlimin might have been twins, and Pehr brother to them both, tall and slender, hairless, with long, graceful limbs that showed none of a Prl'lu's functional knobbiness, and large-eyed, expressive faces, but

where Dunlimin carried no burdens and wore
nothing but dignified Shaper's robes, Talinai
wore a rough jerkin and carried a javelin, fighting stick and spear-quiver that Jak't'rin would
have recognized in an instant—and Phr wore the
armor and weapons Jak't'rin could only dream
of, in such quantities that he was almost lost to
sight beneath layers of harness and armor and
chrome-gleaming armaments.

"We live, do not?" Dunlimin asked.

"Oh, yes, we live," Talinai said, "but Sirunir
does not, and Aslinon does not, and Couilin and
Taneth and Censinar and—how many others?
Admit it, we are none of us in any position to
assume credit." Through all of this exchange
Pehr had remained silent, surveying as much of
their surroundings as the shattered terrain
would let him, his hands near his weapons. He
had assumed the role of warrior and immersed
himself in it completely; it saved him a great deal
of troublesome thinking. Although she bore
weapons as well, that was an attitude Talinai
could not accept. She could not subordinate herself to her weapons; *they* would not die if *she*
failed—but out in the real world she would, as
the machines that contained her and nurtured
her through the tests registered her destruction
and withdrew their protection from her un-
tenanted body.

"Storm," Pehr said. Talinai turned. The sky
along the horizon behind them was black with
thick, rising clouds that boiled and danced with

fierce lightnings in a way that no ordinary storm ever would.

"*Shak'si mir,*" she swore. "We'd best be moving. There's no telling what the Monster's hidden within that mess."

"We'll never outrun that," Dunlimin said.

"Haven't before," Pehr agreed.

"No," Talinai said, "but we might find a place where we'll stand a better chance of living through it. Now let's move."

She felt them die, trapped in her outrage, and she was pleased. She felt the stones kill the two and she felt the footsteps of the third as he fled in madness, not dead yet but no longer a threat, and soon not even a memory.

She listened to the angry conversation of the survivors and took joy in the fear she heard there and then she conjured up yet another storm and hurled it upon them, that they might be assailed even by the very air they breathed.

She was Aquintir; she was the very land they trod and the very world they moved through; and she would be the Shaper to win.

How fortunate I was, she thought, *that when we were bid awaken I was the first, and the first the machines took into themselves, so that I could make the tests my own, and win.*

But it wasn't merely fortune, she knew, She had been the first to awaken because she was the strongest, the most fit, the most deserving to live and rule the Race on this world. The others had been allowed to awaken, of course; that had to be, because there must always be a test, to ensure that the strongest did come to power—but Aquintir would win. She had already reduced more than a hundred challengers to six, and now to three—and soon there would be none, and Aquintir could begin to shape her world.

They almost defeat themselves, she thought. Talinai and Pehr had abandoned the entire reason for a Shaper's existence, taking up arms like Prl'lu and looking for direct physical combat—combat she would never allow them. Dunlimin at least remained true to her heritage—but she made the mistake of choosing to fight Aquintir in her own established concepts. They would fail.

Soon.

A fresh string of missiles impacted high overhead, dusting the men and women in the room with a shower of pebbles and loose grit.

Bannerman Chance cursed as he flinched, then dusted off the plate they stood around. The positions of the surrounded gang were outlined in blue, those of the besieging Prl'lu in pale red. In numbers the humans had an advantage over their attackers, but in almost every other way that mattered, the Prl'lu had the edge. Seventy percent of Chance's gang were noncombatants—wounded, specialists, children, the elderly. The thirty percent that remained—six hundred and thirty-two men and women, were only lightly-armed irregulars, lacking the heavy weapons and transport that might have given them a fighting chance. And yet they hadn't been overrun—

"They're playing with us," Hannah Cauthen said. The pale light of the screen shining up from the table deepened and highlighted the lines that weariness and exhaustion had engraved in all their faces. "They could overrun us at any time. Why don't they?"

"I don't know. Maybe they figure they won't have to. Minelli, what's our stores situation?"

"Assuming we can't set up shop again, and get the processors and the technical people working any time soon, we've got food for maybe a month, medical supplies for half that long—"

"And munitions for about five more days of probing and skirmishing, or one pitched battle. If you can call what it's going to be like when they come for us a battle," Chance finished for him.

"But they haven't come for us yet. Maybe they can't," someone said from back in the cluster.

"Maybe they just don't want to. They aren't even using dis," Chance said. "Has there been any change in our communications situation?"

"None, sir. Jammed on all channels."

"Dammit. Has there been any incoming word on Holcomb's troops?"

Fennering, the phone expert, shrugged. "The last we'd heard before the Prl'lu wrapped up our lines was that he was working out of North Texas somewhere—and he was having troubles of his own."

"Hell, who isn't these days? But we need those troops of his."

"We've got no way to tell him that."

"We've got to find one." Chance ran a hand through his close-cropped, salt-and-pepper hair. It came away feeling grimy. They had been undergoing intermittent shelling from the Prl'lu for four days now and each new onslaught shook down fresh debris from the roofs of the *dis*-hewn deep bunkers. "Have we heard from any of the runners?"

"Not yet." *And we won't*, Fennering's tone seemed to add.

"We've got to get a phone outside this area; we've got to get word to Holcomb—hell, to anybody. We aren't going to get out of this on our own, people."

No one corrected him.

"If I call for volunteers, will I get an answer?"

"You know you will, boss."

Yeah, boss, Chance thought. *I've got scraps of half a dozen gangs here, most of whom didn't know my face from a hole in the ground before the Prl'lu came along. But as long as I'm the one who tells people when and how to go out and get killed, they'll be happy to call me 'boss.' Maybe that's all there ever was to it. . . .*

"The humans are sending out another wave of runners, Commander." Small rectangles of light pinpointed spots on the human lines.

"How many this time?" He touched a button and the world before him fragmented into a shifting series of views of small, scurrying figures.

"Twelve, Commander."

"Neutralize ten at the earliest opportunity. Allow the eleventh to establish but not complete contact."

"Orders regarding the twelfth, Commander?"

"No orders."

Stabs of light and flame cut through the darkness.

Chance crouched in a firing pit, along with the phones officer, looking out into the night, where creatures were trying to kill his people.

"Do you think any of them will make it?" he asked.

"The last five didn't," Fennering said, "and some of these aren't."

"One of them has to," Chance said. "One of them *has* to."

"Oh, Jesus," Holcomb said. "When did this come in?"

"Just now. It was a different operator than the incomplete transmission this morning."

"It would be. The Prl'lu found the other one. My God, what a mess." He played the text back again on the screen before him. "Elements of six gangs, with dependents and noncombatants.

They're surrounded, they're down on stocks and short on transport."

"So what do we do about it?"

Hell. . . . "What else? We're going in after them."

"When are they coming?" Chance asked.

"They didn't give me any numbers, sir," the runner said. "There was no reason to assume that the channel was secure."

"But they said they were coming?"

"Major Holcomb's words were, 'well, we'll have to take care of that, won't we?' "

"That doesn't sound too heavily committed to me," Fennering said.

"What do you want over an unsecured channel?" Chance asked. "A diagram of troop movements? We have to go on the assumption that they are coming. We'll want to have all available transport ready to move at any moment, and we'll want them kept on that status until we know for certain whether we're leaving or not. Same thing for all gang elements, so spread the word. We've got to be ready to get out of here, and anything that isn't ready to move when Holcomb hits those bastards gets left behind. Anything and anybody. Make that clear. This is the only chance we're going to get."

"Commander, the humans are readying their remaining transport."

"Have we located their vehicle concentrations?"

"Yes, Commander."

"Then neutralize them."

Pinpoints of light appeared in the 'sky' before Shak't'kan, outlining the hidden human vehicles. An instant later a second cluster of lights appeared, separating and closing on the first group.

The three heavy transports were the last the gangs had. They had been dug in independently, each in a deep, dis-carved bunker, with almost thirty feet of earth above them.

The smaller sleds and the personnel carriers had been scattered throughout the gang positions, dispersed as widely as possible to avoid any concentration of fire.

The Prl'lu missile salvo walked across the human compound like a chaffing flail through grain. One missile each found a transport, punching deep into the earth. Inertron plating held, but structural members and circuitry were ruined by concussion. Given a month's hard work, enough materials, and sufficient manpower, one of them might be made to fly again.

The other missiles tore at the smaller transport, tearing open bunkers, shattering craft, targeted on the neutrino emissions of the vehicles' power units. By the time the lances of rubied light darted up into the sky and struck

down again from the reflecting satellites, there
was little left for them to hit.

"Jesus Christ," Chance said.

"They knew," Fennering said, "they had to
know, all along. So why the hell did they let our
runners get out?"

"Because we're useful that way," Chance said.
"Holcomb will be coming in, looking to pull us
out of here, and there'll be no way to take us—if
he can get out himself."

"So what can we do?"

"What else? Get the noncombatants into the
deepest bunkers, issue as much of the remaining
ammunition as the troops can carry—and buy as
much time as we can before we lose. . . ."

"I really think we should just leave that thing
alone, Ruth."

"And I don't think we can afford to, Marshal,"
she said. The saloon of the *Wilma Deering* was a
jumble, panelling and terminals missing and
braided wires hanging tied off along the bulk-
heads where systems and parts had been can-
nibalized to repair the damage she had sustained
in her attack on the Prl'lu lunar base.

"You certainly won't get much more use out of
the *Deering*, Marshal," Jefferson's black face was
creased in a scowl. No captain likes to admit his
ship is barely one step up from a derelict. "Not
without an extensive refit that we just can't give
her."

"That—doorway—is the one chance to actually *do* anything for our people that I can think of, Marshal," Harris said.

"*If* we'd be doing anything for them," Rogers said.

"We know we can reach the Prl'lu through it."

"But do we know if we can reach the Prl'lu in North America—or even on the Earth? Can you tell me, Ruth, unequivocally and truthfully, that the Prl'lu base we saw was even on our planet?"

"You know I can't do that, Tony."

"And can you guarantee me that if we turn that device on again, the first thing we see won't be a solid mass of Prl'lu infantry coming through after us?"

"No. I can't promise you that, either."

"Then it stays off. And that wing of the base stays sealed and guarded."

"Dammit, Tony, you're talking more like an old man now than you did when you were eighty-five!" Harris was on her feet now. "You've been thinking about nothing but how to do something about the Prl'lu since they awakened, and now that you've got the chance you're backing off!" She slapped the table-top between them. "We *have* the Prl'lu doorway. Let's use it. If nothing else we can select their bases at random and pump missiles and *dis* through."

"And you think that will help?"

"It can't hurt."

"Even if they decide to do the same back at us?"

Ruth Harris stared at him.

"Even if they're ready to do that right now? You of all people should know how efficient the Prl'lu are, Ruth; you've studied them more than any of us. Do you really think they aren't aware that humans are in control of one of their doorways? They *have* to be ready."

"It's still the only chance we've got."

"It's not enough of a chance. That doorway stays closed, Ruth."

The hatch to the saloon slid open and Peggy Biskani came in, carrying a hard-copy printout from the comm boards up in the control room.

"We've had a tight-beam transmission from Earth, Marshal—from Major Holcomb."

"Thank you." Rogers took the proferred sheet. He started to read it and his face darkened.

"No. Dammit, *no*. Set up for a reply, Peggy. Tell him that he is not, repeat not to undertake this operation."

"We can't do that, Marshal. We lost their carrier-wave immediately upon transmission. They must have started breaking down their lashup as soon as they finished sending. These jury-rigged radio systems aren't all that portable."

"Oh, dear God," was all Rogers could say to that. Ruth Harris reached across and took the message from him.

HOLCOMB COMMANDING BADLANDS GARRISON TO: MARSHAL ROGERS X AM MOVING AGAINST PRLU FORCES SUR-ROUNDING REMNANTS DELAWARES-BAYOU-COASTER-OTHER GANGS IN AR-KANSAS X WILL ADVISE ON RESOLUTION X END XXX

CHAPTER THREE

"The runners report all units in position, Major," the tech said.

"Good." Will Holcomb studied his board. It had taken longer than he would have liked. The Prl'lu jamming had shut down communications all along the spectrum. He had had to position his forces with less communication than Anthony Rogers had enjoyed in the trenches of France, five centuries before. But everything was in order now, or as nearly so as it was ever going to be. "Send a runner to Captain Hopper. Tell him we start the attack on the hour."

"Yes sir."

Holcomb studied the arrangement of his forces on the screen. He was not preparing to fight any kind of lengthy battle. His heavy weapons were positioned to concentrate their fire on one of the Prl'lu units surrounding the trapped gangs; the bulk of his infantry and transport set in one heavy column to punch through in the wake of the barrage. Two smaller units, mobile and well-armed, were set well behind his main body on either flank (at least they should be there— damn that Prl'lu jamming!) to forestall any Prl'lu elements that sought to plug the gap behind him. It was the best he could do.

He checked his chronometer again. In five minutes he would know if it was good enough.

The combat plating slid forward to seal Hopper's Mako, covering the vulnerable canopy. The flyer was entirely cut off from the outside now, save for the evidence of his screens. He knew the same would be happening all around him, as the handful of Makos and Falcons he still commanded locked up for battle. Each ship was heavily laden with ordnance—win or lose this run was going to eat heavily into their remaining stockpiles. He gave little thought to the forthcoming engagement; he knew he could rely on his people, and there was just no predicting the Prl'lu.

He looked at the chronometer before him, the dial reading closer and closer to the jump-off point. He wished the Prl'lu jamming was not so effective; he would have liked to have been able to hear their voices.

Dorothy Chan sat in the sealed-off cockpit of her Mako. Her helmet phones were live but turned well-down, against the constant squeal of Prl'lu jamming. Cool air circulated by the ventilation fans blew gently across the tan forehead and almond eyes visible above her respirator mask.

This was the part she always hated: the long

'moments when you knew something was coming, but there was nothing you could do about it yet, for whatever reason, whoever's fault it was. But hate it as she would, it was always there; it always came down to the waiting.

Then the last numbers on the chrono came up zero and the waiting was over. Dotty Chan punched two buttons and shoved the throttle forward as the Mako's vertical landing thrusters and her cold-rocket booster hurled the ship up and forward, already fast enough for the ship's control surfaces to work. Acceleration punched a great leaden fist into her chest, as though trying to hold her back, warn her away from the carnage she was throwing herself into. . . .

Even as the planes broke free above the treeline the first missiles were cresting the tops of their ballistic arcs and plunging down into the Prl'lu positions. The second wave met a shower of counterbattery fire, bright spears of scarlet light and blue, acid *dis* that stripped away half the salvo's strength before it ever landed—but smoke and flame began to shroud the Prl'lu positions.

The American planes streaked over the Prl'lu, still accelerating. Dotty Chan triggered steady bursts from her rocket cannon, scattering destruction among the running figures on the ground beneath her. Small arms fire began to break against the Mako, but the inertron plating handled it without strain. Ahead of her one of the Prl'lu counterbattery weapons threw up another spray of scarlet light and *dis*. Dotty triggered two powerful SHAPE missiles against the battery, and released two of the three-hundred kilogram bombs from her racks. The position erupted behind her as the Mako rushed past.

Suddenly the jamming was gone from her headphones, and Dotty quickly turned up the gain on a Babel of urgent Prl'lu transmissions and excited human voices.

"Watch that dis battery to the east. Three, can you take it out?"

"Mako Three aknol. Going in."

"Leader to all elements. Stay clear of the western positions. Ground artillery's gunning for them next."

"Falcon Three, Falcon Three—anybody seen Markham?"

"Down on the first pass, Leader. I didn't see him get out."

"Somebody get that sled heading north!"

"Mako Four, aknol," Dotty said. She could just make out the open-cab floater cutting away over the treeline. The little sled couldn't possibly outrun the big pursuit. A burst of cannon fire sent it tumbling in, and she was banking around, back to the battle.

The first wave of human troops hit the Prl'lu. Holcomb had mounted his heavy *dis* units on all his remaining transport. The floaters rushed forward ahead of the armored personnel carriers, their beams slashing at the ground ahead of them, chewing up the Prl'lu positions further. Even armored emplacements suffered, as the ground beneath their supports was cut away and they fell out of line.

But the Prl'lu were not thrown into confusion. What had appeared to be frantic scurrying from the air was actually purposeful, organized troop movements as the Prl'lu dispersed themselves as widely as possible to cover the gaps in their lines and deny the *dis* weapons any concentrated targets.

Jump-belted Prl'lu leaped from the ground toward the incoming sleds. The human crews slashed at them with small arms fire, but more than one sled was lost as an alien warrior landed in the cab and performed slaughter. Groundfire filled the air around the sleds; the open vehicles were far too susceptible to shrapnel and *dis* for a proper combat craft. But they did not have to endure it for long. In seconds they were through the Prl'lu and rushing away over the treetops toward the trapped gangs.

Then the heavier armored personnel carriers arrived. They tore at the defending Prl'lu with SHAPE missiles, cannon and *dis* as they settled and disgorged their squads of infantry. Rocket-belted point troops darted out ahead of the jump-belted men and women following them.

The Prl'lu bore down on them in wave after wave. The rocket-belted troops, caught ahead of the main body, were slaughtered, shot down or pulled from the sky by leaping, jump-belted Prl'lu.

The human infantry quickly formed a perimeter around the hovering carriers, which swivelled and pivoted on their landing jets, bringing their fire to bear on the charging aliens. The infantry fired rapidly, trying desperately to keep the Prl'lu at a distance, trying to keep a corridor open for the trapped gangs.

The Prl'lu returned fire with deadly accuracy, but were forced to refrain from using their heavier weapons because of the close range between the forces. Men and women died, Prl'lu warriors were struck down by precise rocketfire. Once a wedge of Prl'lu troops broke through the human line in a fury of hand-to-hand combat as the American troops drew back frantically, trying to reestablish firing-distance. Finally a mass attack by the armored personnel carriers overwhelmed the Prl'lu infantry in the wedge—but more were coming on. . . .

"Reports indicate that our lines are holding, Major, but we're taking heavy casualties."

"Aknol. We hadn't planned on sticking around here, anyway," Holcomb said. The distant rumbling of explosions reached them through the hull of the ship.

"I just hope those people are ready to move."

"What the hell are you talking about?" the angry lieutenant demanded.

"It's a set-up," Chance repeated. Holcomb's

sleds and floaters were scattered in the fields around him. In the distance, Holcomb's rescue forces were visible only by the rolling columns of smoke rising into the sky. "The Prl'lu knocked out every available piece of transport we had left after our runner got out. They must have known how we'd dispersed them for days. They must have let our man get out to lure you people in here."

"Oh, Jesus . . ."

"Now, listen," Chance said, the words flaying him. "You get on the horn to Holcomb and you tell him to get his people out of here. Tell him it's a trap, set for him. Tell him we can't break out."

The lieutenant hesitated. "We've got some transport here—"

"Not nearly enough."

"We could take *some* of you—"

"Maybe one in twenty. And ninety percent of these people are related to each other. They wouldn't go. Forget it. Get out of here."

But the lieutenant wasn't listening to him anymore. He was staring up at the sky. Chance turned and looked up, and saw the silvery shapes so far above them. . . .

The first of the Prl'lu trapping force came onto the edge of Holcomb's screen just as the first Prl'lu fighting craft were dropping from their carriers. He knew what was happening at once, even before the sled lieutenant's frantic call came in.

He hit the general-channel call-switch. "Holcomb to all units! We've been conned, it's a trap. Start a general withdrawal to the west and start it now. North Flank, brace for an encircling attempt. South Flank, move to reinforce the North. Hopper, try to slow those people down—we need running room. Don't take the time to aknol; just get moving.''

He closed his mike and cursed. This would be bad. He'd never operated this far south before; it was too easy to get pinned against the Gulf. Now it looked as though his fears would be confirmed.

"Get this thing airborne," he ordered. "We're pulling out."

Holcomb's infantry had been pushed back to cover around the grounded carriers. It was the only thing that let them get off. The Prl'lu stormed forward as they began to on-load, fierce and incredibly fast. The carriers couldn't maneuver to direct their fire and take on troops at the same time; within seconds the Prl'lu were on the rearguard and the outermost carriers.

The battle degenerated into a close-order melee, a fight the humans couldn't win against the powerful aliens. A Prl'lu was far more than a match for a human in hand-to-hand fighting. The sleds passed over the bloody tangle as they withdrew from the trapped gangs. They poured *dis* down into the swarming aliens rushing to join the aliens overrunning their companions, but they could do nothing about the Prl'lu already in among the American infantry.

The innermost personnel carriers were lifting off now, and the human line was collapsing inward like a punched paper bag. More than a dozen personnel carriers lay inert on the ground, well behind the advancing Prl'lu. Some of the encircled humans sought to jump clear in long, desperate leaps; others threw themselves upward to be picked up by the passing sleds—but many of the selds that slowed to pick up troops were cut down themselves. Only a handful of the troops still on the ground escaped after the personnel carriers lifted off.

Hopper knew he was going to die.

He had only twelve aircraft left, and most of those had expended much of their ordnance. The Prl'lu had twice that many parent ships; he'd lost count of the smaller fighting craft and transports that were dropping down toward him. If they flew into that hornet's nest, they'd never get out again. But they had to.

He opened his mike. "Hopper to all ships. Forget the big ones up top. Forget the fighters. Go for the transports. They're the ones that'll give our people the most trouble."

An instant later he was among them.

Fire had stabbled down at him from the diving fighters. His Mako had lurched and staggered with the impacts, but their closing speeds had been too great. In seconds he had been past the fighter screen and in among the transports. He had picked out a troop carrier and fired a SHAPE missile into it, done the same with a second—and exhausted what was left of his primary armament. He threw his ship into a tight turn, raking another transport with rocketfire and *dis* as he passed, diving back on his first two targets. Both ships were trailing smoke; so was the Falcon that tumbled past him. *Dis* enveloped his Mako, but it was almost without thought that he cut in his rocket and blew himself clear. Explosions blackened the air around him, but he held to his course and opened up with rockets and *dis* against one of his two cripples, seeking the breach in its armor his SHAPE missile had to have made. He closed on the transport, firing steadily—and suddenly the smoke from the transport thickened, and he could see flame pouring from its flank, and it veered off and fell out of formation, spinning slowly.

He stamped rudder and threw himself around after his second target. Again explosions and *dis* clawed at his ship, again he opened fire, seeking his original wound. He was still three hundred meters from the transport when his rocket cannon went silent, but he continued to close, slashing at the Prl'lu ship with *dis*. A moment later it began to fall back from its position in formation, and small figures began to tumble from beneath, to float gently toward the ground on jump belts. Hopper dove after them, *dis* playing out ahead of the Mako. It was butchery, and he knew it—but he was never going to get out of this to be called to task for it and every one of those monsters that reached the ground was a threat to his people.

Suddenly a giant's fist struck at the Mako and half the readouts on Hopper's boards went red. An instant later an enormous black shape swept past his plane and miles into the distance before it could begin its long, wide turn.

Hopper fought for control of his crippled ship as the Prl'lu fighter came back after him, finally getting it balanced precariously on its landing thrusters. His engines were gone. His own *dis* beam was out of commission. If he jumped the Prl'lu ship would finish him in passing; if he rode the crippled Mako down it would be to land in territory the Prl'lu infested.

His rocket-boost thruster still had pressure.

Hopper waited, calmly, until the Prl'lu ship had committed itself to its attack run. He hit the rocket just as the first fire leaped out ahead of his attacker. The fighter was approaching him at a good three times the speed of sound. His rocket was boosting him forward with a full four gravities of acceleration. The impact was spectacular, if anybody had been watching.

Dotty Chan pulled her Mako wide, away from the burning ships and the dying friends, fighting for control with one engine gone and the port ailerons not responding with any kind of precision. The board in front of her was cross-hatched in red; the Mako was staying in the air out of little more than habit. The ship was crabbing slowly north and east, down two thousand feet already and still dropping. But the battle zone was a good thirty kilometers behind her, and nobody seemed to have the time to pursue and finish off one cripple.

She gave up on the damaged ailerons, locking them in place and compensating for the drag with several degrees of flaps cranked in. She compared her compass and what course her eyes told her she was actually flying and was reassured. She was in a strong northerly current; if she could avoid losing altitude she could as a last resort trip in her landing jets and coast with the wind.

The battle around Holcomb's trapped forces was a dark smudge on the distant horizon. Dotty felt a moment's irrational regret at abandoning them, and suppressed it sharply. She was flying a limping cripple with no ordnance left; there was nothing she could possibly have done.

Now she had to give consideration to her own situation. The ship was maintaining altitude and heading, but she had nowhere to go. Holcomb's troops had been one of the last organized forces on the continent. She could never make it to the holdouts on the Mexican border; to do so she would have had to reverse course and pass too closely to the battle behind her for safety. She didn't know where or even if any other forces still operated, but she did know that if she maintained her course she would be heading into the American northeast, into a region of the country where the gangs had been most numerous. If she grounded there, she supposed, her chances for linking up with stragglers or being able to scrounge a decent living on the land would be better than anywhere else, however slim.

"The attack progresses, Commander. The human warriors are attempting to withdraw to the west. Our units are maintaining contact and moving to encircle them."

"Good," Shak't'kan said. "What is the status of the incident at the transit station?"

"The guard on duty is healing. There have been no further attempts by the humans to activate their end of the system. We have yet to track down their station of origin."

"Discontinue such efforts. You will not locate them unless they attempt to make use of their transit point again. Report on the progress of the countermeasures ordered."

"A wide-bore diffuser had been installed in alignment with our transit point, and set to be triggered by activation of our unit. Installation of additional armoring in the transit chamber proceeds, and the corridor and level entry blast doors are still in place."

"Very well," Shak't'kan said. "Report again as ordered."

He turned his attention back to the view ahead of him. The observation chamber was looking out from the perspective of one of his atmospheric fighters as it closed on a fleeing human armored personnel carrier. Something too fast to be clearly defined leaped ahead of the Prl'lu ship. The carrier was lost briefly in a cloud of flame, and then reappeared, tumbling chaotically toward the ground below.

It was nearly finished.

The American withdrawal had fast become a rout. Holcomb had watched, sickened, as the Prl'lu forces struck against his rearguard elements and continued onward with no lessening of pace. More Prl'lu ships had appeared to the north, rushing after them, trying to cut them off from open country and pin them against the Gulf.

The command transport was grounded, for a short time, while the communications systems were deployed to give Holcomb some idea of what was happening.

The Prl'lu seemed to be everywhere, he thought sickly. The communications bands were growing progressively thicker with transmissions in the harsh, alien tongue, and less crowded by human voices. Once in a while he would hear one of his units being cornered and turning to make a stand—but he never heard from any of them a second time.

"We've heard as much as we're going to hear," he told the techs. "Let's button up again and get out of here."

"Yes, Major."

Holcomb opened the intercom.

"Lieutenant, we'll be lifting off as soon as all

the hardware's back aboard. You folks had better get ready up there."

"*Aknol, Ma*—" Holcomb felt the shock as the cockpit windshield was blown inward and the flight crew died.

The tech standing by the open hatchway turned at the blast—and died as a spear of light pierced her body. There was a series of whistling reports from a human rocket-pistol outside, followed by a string of sharp explosions, suddenly stopped. Holcomb knew he wouldn't see the other techs again.

Then he was bolting from his seat and reaching for his own pistol as the Prl'lu troops flooded into the transport. He got off one shot as those tall, angular warriors towered up over him. He was never sure which struck him first, the concussion from the explosion or the clubbed Prl'lu gun-butt. But he remembered nothing after that.

The storm was upon them, and with it, horror.

They had fled the darkening clouds across the torn plains, knowing they could not outrun them, but looking for shelter where they might possibly survive the coming storm.

They had found it, they thought, a great overhanging shelf of stone jutting at a forty-five-degree angle from the ruined earth. They had thrown themselves beneath it just as the sky went black with roiling cloud above them.

Wind struck at Talinai, Dunlimin and Pehr

like a breaking wave, washing around them,
seeking to drive them back. Rain struck at them,
thicker than rain should have been, and warm as
blood.

And the things came out of the storm, and at
them, leaping, slithering, bounding across the
earth already become mire, legion and beyond
description and each wanting the three Shapers
dead.

Talinai readied a javelin. Pehr drew forth his
gleaming weapons and locked down his visor.

And Dunlimin put forth her will.

The torrent of horror thundering toward them
split as a stream might part around an obdurate
boulder. The creatures hurling themselves at
Dunlimin were suddenly turned, jostling against
their mates, stumbling and blundering against
one another—and headed straight for Talinai
and Pehr.

Flame and light and thunder lashed out from
the chromed metal in Pehr's hands; the nightmares before him crisped and blackened and fell
screaming. Talinai hurled her javelin, spitting
the soft, gibbering impossibility that reared up
on segmented hindquarters before her. Then she
drew short spear and fighting stick and threw
herself against the things facing her. Lightning
cracked and thunder rumbled as she plunged
into their midst.

Pehr's weapons blazed as he moved forward
into the swarming obscenities before him.
Talinai hacked and spun and slashed, the sheer

numbers of the beasts around her presenting her with a wall of flesh impossible to miss, and hampering their own attacks.

Dunlimin stood her ground beneath the overhanging rock, one hand extended in a gesture of warding. With the other she reached above her head and made a fist, then jerked it down. Lightning plummeted from the storm clouds above and tore at shrieking creatures held at bay before her.

The battle seemed to rage for hours. More than once clubbed fist or claw or grasping tendril found their mark, but Talinai cut and slashed at each as it came and remained free and upright, killing things that never should have lived. She buried the blade of her short spear in something with too many arms and far too many teeth—and stepped back in horror as something huge and black and hard-edged as the stone around them seemed to rise up out of nowhere, dwarfing and scattering the lesser foulnesses around it. It seemed to grow until its square head creased the bottoms of the clouds overhead, and looked down with eyes that glowed with an unclean, greenish-white luminance in its shadowed face. It stooped to reach down for her—

—and its great, blunt-fingered hand burst apart as the light from Pehr's weapons struck into it. The black titan seemed to arch back in astonishment as the Shaper in warrior's armor stepped forward, his weapons held before him and firing without stopping, pouring their energy now into the titan's breast, where it built and accumulated until the stony flesh of the giant began to glow with a light of its own.

And then the colossus shattered, in an explosion that rivalled the thunder around them. Stone flew in every direction, and the two Shapers were cast to the ground by the shock.

As they sought their feet hastily, they could see that the field around them was empty again, save for the charred, hacked corpses of the creatures they had felled. The rubble of the titan was indistinguishable from the granite spires around them.

They turned back toward Dunlimin—and stood transfixed as the granite shelf gave a single convulsive heave and plunged down atop the Shaper. She hadn't even had the time to register surprise.

Around them, the cutting wind of the storm seemed to shriek with madman's laughter.

Aquintir laughed in delight. With Dunlimin's death a weight had lifted from her mind, a pressure against the reality she maintained, in which she held primacy. Only the lesser weight of Pehr and Talinai still remained, and when they were gone she would be supreme, and the machines would have to acknowledge it, would have to stop the warning spikes of pain, and allow her to awaken to take her part in the creation of a world. . . .

*   *   *

The square Prl'lu script flowed up the screen, each listing a possibility, each possibility forbidden.

Ruth Harris studied the listings. The Prl'lu doorway behind her was dark, inert; she was not ready to take that step yet. But she would.

Holcomb's defeat had very nearly broken Anthony Rogers, as well. As long as there had been at least some American forces still free in the field, he could promise himself that there was still some chance, that something might yet be done to thwart the Prl'lu. But now he couldn't tell himself that any longer. He had run out of options, and illusions about those options. Ruth Harris knew Anthony Rogers. It was only a matter of time before he ordered the *Deering* back to Earth and got himself killed, and the Earth's last faint hopes died along with him.

She knew one setting she already couldn't risk, from experience. But how to choose the one she wanted now? There was no way of telling what settings led where. She only knew, with a surety she could never have justified aloud, that their last choice of action lay on the other side of that glowing door, away from this crippled base on a dead moon.

The hell with it, she thought. If one setting was as good as another, she might as well go with the top of the list. The first selection in column was highlighted as she punched out her choice. Then she turned her attention to the operator's boards.

*   *   *

Jak't'rin lay on his back, staring up at the stars, deeply troubled.

He believed his words to Chen't'kin; it was the duty of the Blood to preserve the Prl'an through their time alone, to hone them and purify them as they honed and purified this raw world they had been given. When they had carried out that duty, then and only then would the Shapers awaken to lead them forward into glory.

But Chen't'kin had believed in *his* words, as well—that it was past time for the Shapers to appear, that the Blood had fulfilled its responsibilities as well as it ever would. And the villages grew slowly these days, if at all: no new settlements had been begun in Jak't'rin's lifetime, and the fields expanded but little. Few more young were born than oldsters died each year and of those few, fewer still were taken into the ranks of the Blood. . . .

He had been right to kill Chen't'kin, Jak't'rin knew—but had Chen't'kin also been right to challenge him?

Enough, he thought, as the bright pinpoint of the Waking Star rose above him and sped swiftly across the night sky. *I will make pilgrimage to Hrak'un'Mrak one more time, to look upon its perfection and prove to myself that I have served truly.*

His eye was drawn to the bright blue light of the Evening Star, fleeing over the far horizon in advance of the coming sun, and he envied that tranquil glow its uncompromised simplicity.

CHAPTER FOUR

The compound was not at all bad, certainly not as inhuman as Holcomb had thought it would be.

Apparently the Prl'lu felt little need to continually remind their victims of their oppression. The compound was clean, and well-plumbed, with ample if spartan accomodation. Of course, a large part of that spaciousness was caused by the few humans that dwelled there. This was a compound for military prisoners, and there were less than two thousand of them.

The Prl'lu commander with the sharp, difficult name had made the reason for that abundantly clear.

"The ones who live are the ones who should have lived," Shak't'kan said. "They are the ones who fought."

"And the ones who didn't fight?" Holcomb asked.

Shak't'kan shrugged, an oddly human gesture. "They were of no value."

"No value? Even the noncombatants? Even the god-damned children?" Holcomb could feel the anger building, and knew he was about to get himself killed when he threw himself at the Prl'lu before him—

Shak't'kan had stared at him uncomprehendingly for an instant. Then: "*Of course* we spared the noncombatants. What is the point of slaughtering useful workers?"

"Then where are they?"

"Other compounds. One does not house workers with warriors."

"And what do you intend to do with my people here?" Holcomb asked.

"They are not your people anymore. You are ours; that is the definition of victory. And we shall do with you what you make it possible for us to do with you."

"What do you mean?"

"We have many thousands of your workers in captivity. We can defeat them easily, kill them in numbers you could not comprehend, if we so chose. But we cannot police them."

"And you want us to do it. You want us to be your trustees."

"There is nothing else for you. Understand this; you have lost. This is no longer your world. But there may yet be a place in it for you. I would not deny your courage. You have resisted us bravely, and more successfully than you know. But you have lost, and now I would offer you a chance to stop fighting honorably and resume your stewardship of your workers."

"I can't say it isn't tempting, at this point," Holcomb answered. "It isn't as if we have much choice."

"Then you will resume your stewardship."

"It isn't that simple. I'll have to place this proposal—"

"It is not a proposal."

"—and there will be opposition if I present it as an ultimatum," Holcomb continued. "Many of these warriors were never under my direct command. I will have to convince them to accept this offer."

"You are the ranking human officer in this compound. They have no choice but to accept you," Shak't'kan said.

"I'm the ranking officer in a defeated army," Holcomb said. "We're not like you in these things. You should know that by now; if you don't, we'll be useless to you."

Shak't'kan seemed to consider this, briefly. "Very well. Perhaps it would be best then if we were to have an intermediary in this, one who knows us each better than we might understand each other, as yet." He touched a button on the panel beside him. "Send him in."

The door at the far end of the slender ramp opened—and Mordred walked in, to stop and stare at the human facing him.

With an effort, Holcomb maintained his calm as he turned back to Shak't'kan.

"You do have a lot to learn," he said.

"What the hell am I supposed to do with you?" Holcomb asked.

"You could listen to me," Mordred said. He wore a shapeless set of Alliance fatigues from captured stores. A human of Asiatic ancestry would be just another Prl'lu prisoner. A captured Han would be dead in an hour. "You have to start thinking in terms of the options these demons give you. You've already failed at your own choices."

"Some options. Assuming these people agree to the Prl'lu offer, it'll finish us for sure. Instead of a couple of thousand troops in one place, they'll have us in nice, bite-sized chunks scattered all over the continent, merrily hated by the gangs we're supposed to be policing. We'll never have chance of doing anything then."

"You haven't got a chance of doing anything *now*," Mordred said. "You're beaten, Major. You know it and the Prl'lu certainly do. They don't even guard this compound. At least their offer will give you some chance of looking after your gangs' interest. It isn't your world, anymore. Get used to that."

"You're pretty quick to fold up, all of a sudden," Holcomb said. "That's the one thing no one could ever say against you before."

"Before I was fighting something I had a chance against," Mordred said. "The demons are different. The sooner you realize that, the better off you'll be." He held up a hand to forestall Holcomb's reply. "You've been lucky, so far. The demons respect you because you gave them as much of a fight as you did. But may whatever gods you care to pray to protect you if you ever provoke them too far. They have—ways—of maintaining discipline, and I can speak from experience and promise you they're effective."

"So give in to them; is that your advice?"

"Accept their power for now, yes, because it's very, very real. And try to maintain some kind of organization under their rule, something that can be used against them some day, if you have to justify it to yourself like that. You humans seem to be very good at that. But don't try to fight them now, unless you want to guarantee butchery. Your own."

There was an explosion, far behind her, as the Prl'lu trackers destroyed her grounded fighter.

Dotty Chan pushed on northward, in short, low jumps that kept her well beneath the tree-line. The Prl'lu fighter had caught her unexpectedly over old Pennsylvania. It had had time only for one pass at its high speed, then she was wrestling what was left of her Mako down between the trees. She had fled on foot before the ship could return, but she had seen the sled it dropped as he belted away, and the tall figures riding it down.

Now they were hunting her.

Her chances as she reasoned them weren't too poor against the trackers on the ground—considering that she had no idea where to seek help, only two magazines for her pistol, and the few days' rations in her survival kit—although she knew she would have to turn and face them eventually. But the sled was a definite threat. It was coming on swiftly above the trees, and she felt sure it possessed instruments that would pierce her forest cover with ease. That would have to be her first priority.

She checked her flight in the branches of a tall oak, bracing herself against the heavy trunk, drawing her pistol. Working carefully, alert to the danger of dropping anything, she withdrew the butt-plate and threaded, extensible stock from her kit and fastened them in place.

The sled was keeping to a straight course, which convinced her that they were using instruments. She raised her pistol to her shoulder, both hands tight on the grip, and tried to allow for the sled's course and altitude. She fired once, twice, a third time, bracketing her aiming point. There was an explosion in the distance and she was moving again, uncertain whether her attack had succeeded but not willing to stick around and find out. . . .

They had left the shattered plains behind them three days ago. Talinai and Pehr climbed now, through a series of low foothills that presaged the towering peaks still gray in the distance.

"There is a thing we have not spoken of," Pehr said, not taking his eyes from their path.

"Is there?"

"Indeed. We contest against the monster Aquintir, who bests us at every turn. But have you considered that if we should triumph against her, we will yet have to contest against each other?"

"That seems a distant enough possibility that I will not worry about it," Talinai said, digging in the haft of her javelin for purchase. "We are all that remains of a hundred and more, no less capable than ourselves, all slain already. The prospect of our surviving to do murder against each other seems small."

Pehr reached for an outcropping, pulled himself up again, his weapons and armor clattering. "Then you do not believe we can succeed?"

"The prospect seems small," Talinai repeated.

"But it is not utterly impossible."

"If it comforts you to think of it in those terms; no, it is not."

"That will have to be enough," Pehr decided soberly.

"We will not get anything more. It is strange," Talinai said, "I should have thought a world would offer room enough for more than one Shaper. It seems pointless to destroy one another when such a challenge awaits us."

"Aquintir does not seem to think so," Pehr said. "And as she wills, so things seem to be here."

"Yes." They had reached the crest of the hill. The foothills stretched on beyond them under a clear sky, void of any threat. "And yet it has been three days since she last attacked. Perhaps her thinking changes."

*   *   *

Aquintir screamed her denial and fought the machines with all her will.

This latest attack had been the worst yet since the machines had analyzed her strategy. They were trying to take her world from her, to force her down into the test on the same level as Talinai and Pehr, to deny her her rightful power.

The machines thought her mad, a deviate. In their flat, impersonal voices they tried to reason with her, to lull her suspicions while they sought to break her hold on the world she had created through them. They spoke of *non-optimal involvement* and *scenario distortion* and *biased premises*—but what they meant was that even they feared her, and knew her to be too strong for them, and wanted to bring her down.

Never! She screamed, deep in her mind. *I am not your servant! This test is here to be won, by whatever means, and I will win it!*

But the machines only continued their monotonous droning, and tried again and again to work subtle wedges between her mind and the world she had made within it. . . .

"You aren't going to like this, Marshal."

"Captain Jefferson, there are a great many things in this life that I don't like, but I've had it borne in on me that I can't do a damned thing about most of them. What is it now?"

"We've located Doctor Harris, sir."

Rogers looked up, suddenly apprehensive. "Where?"

"Apparently she's made use of the Prl'lu doorway—"

"What?"

"We found the system activated and the doorway open, sir, and there's no sign of her anywhere else in the base."

"Dammit," Rogers swore. "I should have known better than to try and give an order to a *Deering* woman. Is anyone else missing?"

"No, sir. And I've posted guards on the doorway."

"Good. Let's get down there."

The doorway opened onto shadow. Faint light came from somewhere to one side of the roughly-cut stone visible through the *dis* beam; the rock walls and floorway bore no fixtures or markings.

As he walked around the doorway, studying it, Rogers noticed that it was more like a column than a doorway. His view of the chamber on the other side changed as he circled it, and now he could see the lighted panels of a unit not unlike the one on their side.

"Captain, have any of your people touched any of the settings on this thing?"

"No, Marshal."

"Good." He stood before the doorway, glaring at it unhappily. "Well, I suppose the good doctor hasn't left us a great many options, has she?" He drew his pistol and chambered a round.

"Let me send a party through first, Marshal."

"No, thanks, Captain. Your people can at least help run the *Deering* and keep this base operating. I'm the resident fifth wheel at the moment." He turned to look at Jefferson. "Keep the guard on this doorway and have one man always stationed on the unit power switch. That's the lower button, over there," he added, pointing. "If anything—anything at all—tries to come through the machine that isn't Doctor Harris or myself, cut the power and do not restore it. Is that clear?"

"Sir—"

"Is that clear?"

"Yes, Marshal."

"Good. See you in a bit."

He stepped into the field.

He hadn't known what to expect, but it didn't feel at all unpleasant. There was a faint, clinging sensation, as though he was trying to force his way through the skin of a soap bubble, and a slight chill. Then he was through, standing alone in the shadowed corridor. The faint light he had seen from beyond the doorway came from another chamber around a short, curving corridor. By the light of the panels of the doorway system on this side, he could see that all the walls were the same bare stone, roughly hewn by *dis* to form the chamber. Except for the unit, the room was empty.

Gun in hand, he moved toward the lighted chamber. It proved to be only a small anteroom before a sliding door, with no other features— except for the small stylus, of familiar human manufacture, that had been placed very carefully on the floor, tip pointing straight through the closed door.

Rogers knelt and picked up the stylus. It had obviously been placed, not dropped, not the way it pointed right at the door.

For a moment he considered simply getting to his feet, opening the door, and barging through into whatever might await him. He had no further responsibilities back on the Moon, and none he could fulfill back on Earth. It was a temptation to assume that whatever happened would happen, and plunge ahead. But he still had one obligation to honor—his obligation to Ruth Harris. She had reactivated the doorway in spite of his order because it was the one way she could think of to help him, he knew that; and whatever she faced now she was facing because of Anthony Rogers. He owed it to her not to go off half-cocked.

He turned and made his way back to the glowing doorway. He felt the clinging sensation as he passed through again, but this time he felt a flush of warmth as he stepped through into the lunar chamber.

Jefferson was still there, and the guards, with weapons half-levelled.

"Get a party together, Captain," Rogers said. "Leave one person to tend ship, one to guard that switch. I want everyone else, with weapons, armor and rations. Doctor Harris is in there somewhere, and we're going in after her."

Jefferson grinned. "Aknol," he said, and left

the chamber. It was the first time Rogers had heard the slang agreement in weeks. *We're finally doing something,* he told himself, *that's what it is. We may get killed, but at least we're not just sitting around waiting for it.* And he found himself grinning as he left the room for his own gear.

"*Shak'si mir!*" Jak't'rin cursed.

He stood at the top of the low bowl-valley that should have encircled Hrak'un'Mrak—but Hrak'un'Mrak was no longer there.

Where once it had stood, a flawless hemisphere of mirrored silver perfect in its simplicity, there squatted a utilitarian structure of plain gray stone, adorned with strange devices and structures Jak't'rin could not recognize.

He was numbed by the blasphemy of it, by this gross usurpation of the very heart of his faith. Hrak'un'Mrak was *forever,* it had been the central facet of history and myth for generations of the Blood, the bright promise of glory to come when they had earned it. And now, to find it replaced by *this*—

Before he knew it he was running, leaping down the slope into the valley, javelin carried high before him, his encumbering bedroll abandoned. He did not know who might be the masters of this gross edifice, but whoever they were, they would answer to him. . . .

All was darkness about Aquintir.

The testing systems were loyal to their programming, and fought tirelessly to rid the tests of her distortion. Aquintir was stubborn but she was not invincible. At her least hesitation, her slightest mistake, the correcting programs struck again, dislodging her just that little bit more from her grip on the test's reality. The world she had helped to shape was a faint luminance in the distance now, a small islet of light in an ocean of blackness.

She was losing it, she knew; she was losing the only world she had, and her one chance to Shape another. She could not bear it.

She would not bear it.

She screamed—and rode that scream up out of the blackness, a psychic banshee wailing for death yet to come. The blackness tore at her, eroding her, wearing her away from without as the scream consumed her from within. She was calm, tranquil in her singularity of purpose. She would win back to her world or she would die, torn apart by the systems' restraints.

The light of the world grew brighter as she drew near—but she was fast becoming less aware of it. She was attenuating, thinning out, the stuff of her self being spent too quickly in her shrieking flight. She felt the dissolution as it progressed, but paid it no attention. If she won through to her world, she would be whole again. If she did not . . . it would not matter.

The light was spreading wider and wider as she drew nearer; it was growing fainter and fainter as she lessened.

She was almost there, now; the world was less

than a hand span away as she stretched to grasp it, less than a fraction of the self that had been, driven on only by an insane will that would not be denied.

But that will was not enough.

The scream wavered and went soft; the hand she extended raked at the edge of the world and left evaporating wisps of perceived flesh behind as it fell back. The world began to dissolve away as her perception of it failed, like smoke borne away on a breeze.

The scream died—

—and the world was real beneath her again, rock and earth and sky, and she could see the whole of it and feel the whole of it and rule the whole of it once again. She had beaten the machines. The restraining of a mad Shaper had been beyond their programmed limits: in the end they had known only that a Shaper was about to die directly because of them, rather than as part of the selection between Shapers—and that was something they were entirely forbidden. So they had yielded, and submitted to Aquintir's will, and given her back the world.

She put forth her senses once again, and felt the featherlight footsteps of her last two arrogant challengers. Then she struck, free at last to remove them without hindrance.

Aquintir's rage boiled down out of the mountains in a solid wall of wind and hail. The storm clawed Pehr off his precarious perch on the hillside and sent him rolling and clattering down the slope.

Talinai bent her head as the hail punched and stabbed at her, then turned and half-scrambled, half-fell back down the way she had come. Pehr was just lurching to his feet as she reached the bottom of the slope, his armor battered, his helmet askew.

"No, she hasn't changed her thinking," Talinai shouted above the howl of the wind. She doubted that Pehr had heard her; he just waved an arm ahead of them, indicating that they should seek shelter. They moved out quickly, hurrying to stay ahead of whatever might follow in the storm.

They reached a point where the gully they followed hooked sharply; around the bend, the wind was partially blocked and the hailstones merely fell instead of being driven.

"This is madness," Talinai cried.

"Yes," Pehr answered her flatly.

"We cannot see her, we cannot speak to her, we do not even know where to seek her!"

"Then what is the point of this?"

"The point is, we have failed," Pehr said. "And now she means to kill us."

"What sort of test is that?"

"One she has beaten us at," Pehr said. "Listen."

Above the wind, they heard the distant howling of beasts.

"Again?" Talinai moaned.

"This time Dunlimin is not here to oppose her. This time she can devote her full energies to us."

"Then we cannot win."

"Not the two of us, no," Pehr said. He stood and looked around them. "Try to circle around this hill and move on. They will not follow soon."

"Why won't they?"

"I will be here."

"Then they will kill you!"

"But not both of us."

"This is madness again!"

"I do not agree. We have failed so far because we have each fought for ourselves alone, Dunlimin for Dunlimin, I for myself, you for yours, all the others, each for themselves. Did none of us ever consider that fighting together against the Monster might be more important? Would Couilin have broken if there had been any to share his fear? Perhaps it is too late to correct our errors now, but I will make them no more." He drew his weapons and turned his back on her. "Now go."

He clambered onto a low spire of rock, from which he could dominate the narrow valley. By the time he turned and looked back, she was gone.

The reports from Pehr's weapons reached Talinai from halfway around the hill. She hesitated for a moment, then turned and fought her way back against the cutting wind, searching for a vantage point.

Pehr stood out briefly at each flash of his weapons, reflected off bright body armor. The gully before him writhed and twisted with the unholy life that infested it, life that blocked up in front of his position and then resumed its advance, slowly, in bits and pieces, as scattered creatures fought their way through his fire and towards his position.

They were climbing toward him, now, a wave of darkness that oozed its way up the rock spire. He shifted his fire then, directing it downward into the mass rising up toward him, but it was never enough. He slaughtered nightmares without number but there were always more, rising up toward him.

Then the black wave crested the spire and overwhelmed him. There was one last glint of chrome as he fired, struggling to throw off the things that gripped his arms and legs and sought to bring him down.

Then he was gone.

Talinai watched the seething, obscene swarm for several seconds, then turned and resumed her progress around the hill.

They had run Dotty Chan as far as she was going to be run.

Her position was good, using the wall of the streambed as a parapet, concealed by the thick

shrubbery there. She watched up the path she
had come, but she knew better than to assume
the Prl'lu would use the open trail. She kept her
attention focussed on the undergrowth to either
side of the path.

· She heard them before she could see them.
Even the best woodsman cannot avoid the scuf-
fled leaves and the snapped branches of an in-
cautious footfall, but the aliens were very good.
If she had not been listening for them she might
have assumed it was merely random forest noise.

Then she saw them—first one, then a second,
then the third. The others were behind them, she
knew that although she wasn't sure how many
more there might be, but she couldn't wait any
longer.

The first one died instantly as a rocket caught
it cleanly in the chest; then she was swinging her
weapon and chewing up the woods around
another, already in motion, seeking cover and a
firing point. The others were charging now,
three of them, five, as she tried to swing her
weapon back into line and saw the muzzles of
strange guns bearing on her—

—fire clawed at the Prl'lu from their upstream
flank, explosions and solid-slug projectiles that
tore at them and cut them down even as they
turned to meet this new threat. One of the aliens
sent a shaft of scarlet light cutting into the
woods, shredding saplings and underbrush,
scarring thicker trees deeply. Somewhere a man
screamed. Then the alien fell. With terrible vital-

ity two of the Prl'lu were crawling after weapons
torn from their grasp by concussion. There was
another eruption of fire around them, and when
the dust had cleared, they lay still.

Dotty pivoted then, bringing her pistol to bear
in the direction of the Prl'lu that had tried to
outflank her. She didn't have far to look. He
swung gently from a shrapnel-torn tree, suspended from the stump of a broken branch by the
sling of his weapon. His dead face bore an expression of utmost astonishment.

Dotty Chan relaxed then, and waited. Whoever her unseen rescuers were, they would be
coming to see what they had saved next.

There was a rustling of branches and Dotty
Chan's eyes widened in surprise.

They stood there, perhaps a dozen of them,
men and women, slight of stature and dark of
skin, with straight black hair and large, dark,
markedly epicanthic eyes. They wore worn
clothing of no common origin and carried a mot-
ley collection of human weapons, small arms of
unfamiliar make, even some Prl'lu weapons—
more of the latter now, as several of her rescuers
went to work stripping the dead Prl'lu of
weapons and kit.

One of the strangers stepped forward, a young
woman with long, dark hair, who carried a com-
pact solid-slug automatic weapon slung over
one shoulder, and wore a tattered set of Alliance
field coveralls.

"Welcome," she said. "You've brought us no

little profit today, whoever you are." Her English was good but accented.

"I'm glad I had someplace to bring it," Dotty Chan said. "But just who have I brought it to?"

"You have a short memory for an Alliance officer," the woman said, "particularly considering how so many of you were ready to go to war over me some months ago."

"No," Dotty said, realization dawning.

"Oh, yes," the once-Princess Lu-An said.

"Welcome to the last stronghold of the Han."

CHAPTER FIVE

They crouched and levelled their weapons as Rogers reached for the door-switch. It slid aside silently as he threw himself back—to reveal emptiness.

Oh, the large room beyond the door had held something, at one time—but not now. The rows upon rows of Prl'lu stasis cylinders, identical to the ones at the lost Antarctic base, were all open and empty, their occupants gone to . . . where-ever.

Rogers and the party from the *Deering* moved carefully through the room, and the room beyond that and the next—and that was where they came upon the machines.

It looked a Prl'lu museum of war. Machines the humans had only seen briefly on Earth, as the Prl'lu used them against them, and machines the likes of which men had never seen before; they were all there, monolithic in their size and power—and every one of them immobile, un-manned.

Rogers pushed off and belted to the top of one of the great fighting vehicles, to land atop a secondary turret sprouting a gun muzzle wider than the primary armament of the *Wilma Deering*. There were three columns of such vehicles in the room, and no sign of any crew—or Ruth Harris. He considered risking an ultrophone call, then decided against it: there had been a lot of Prl'lu in those empty cyclinders, one time or another, and he sure as hell didn't want to let them know that they had uninvited company.

He dropped back down to the waiting party.

"I don't see anybody here nursemaiding these things," he said, "but let's not take any chances. Captain, there are more vehicles to either side of us, with two more aisles between them. Put flanking parties in each aisle, not to fire or make any transmissions unless absolutely necessary. If we do run into anything, the drill is to sound off and hightail it back to the doorway, clear?"

"Aknol, Marshal. Biskani and Johnson, left aisle. Howell and Podres, to the right."

"Aknol." The four crewmembers moved off between the machines.

"All right," Rogers said, "let's move out."

They made their way down the aisle, walking, refraining from using their belts. The massive Prl'lu ordnance passed silently to either side of them.

Jak't'rin paused uncertainly outside the great structure that had supplanted Hrak'un'Mrak.

He had run down into the valley, fueled by indignation and righteousness—and he had no idea what to do next. He had no idea what manner of strange beings could possibly abort the permanence of Hrak'un'Mrak. And he had no idea how properly to challenge them.

He circled cautiously around the building. There was no challenge from within, no sign that he had been noticed. He had found only the one great door, a dozen times as high as a warrior and broad enough for his entire village to have walked through it abreast. There seemed to be no other way in or out.

He studied the lintels of the great doorway. They were free of any superficial adornment— save for the one plate of gleaming metal with the two disks embedded in it.

Jak't'rin studied the plate carefully, then reached out and touched the topmost of the two disks. It yielded slightly, tempting him to press harder—

The great doors pivoted silently outward, revealing a chamber whose innermost reaches were lost in shadow. He levelled his javelin and stepped through, into the half-darkness.

The only light in the great chamber came from thin strips, widely spaced overhead, that glowed with a blue-white radiance cooler than that of the sun. The chamber was empty, otherwise.

He pushed inward, toward the shadows at the far end of the room, shadows broken by a broad shaft of daylight from the open doors. The thin seam of another doorway was visible in the infiltrating light.

He walked up to the doors and edged sideways

into the shadows, feeling for the frame. His theory was justified; his hand found another metal panel, identical to the first, with identical disks. He pressed the topmost disk. The doors opened, sliding away into the wall this time, and the explosion threw him back into the shadows.

"Prl'lu!" Jefferson shouted, and raised his rifle. But Rogers was already firing. The tall alien spun back out of sight in the blast.

The party had scattered around them, seeking cover among the great machines. At a gesture from Jefferson, two frontmost crewmembers started forward as the two flanking parties appeared from their aisles and raced to either side of the doorway, weapons ready.

The first crewman was scant meters from the door when a tall figure leaped into view. The long arm above its head whipped down, and the crewman grunted and fell back at the impact of the long javelin against his armor. The flanking parties stepped out into the open, firing rapidly—but the Prl'lu was gone, and their rockets scored only stone flooring.

Rogers and the rest of the crew rushed forward.

"How many of them are there?" Rogers demanded.

"I only saw the one, Marshal," Biskani answered, her eyes on the room before them.

"He could be alone," Jefferson said.

"And he could not," Rogers answered. "Anybody see anything?"

"I thought I heard something," Biskani said. "Over there."

"Put a round into the corner, see what happens."

Biskani knelt and raised her weapon. The rest of the crew took cover behind the doorframe or went prone and levelled their weapons.

Biskani fired into the darkness—and the rest of the crew opened fire as Jak't'rin threw himself through the open outer doors. Gunfire stitched around him as he ran; the door at his side shuddered at the impact of a rocket.

He reached the edge of the door and threw himself around it, rolled to his feet and kept running for the treeline, not slowing until he was a hundred meters deep into the woods.

Then he allowed himself to fall to his knees and rest. It was one of the few failings of the Prl'lu metabolism that it produced energy so efficiently—and thereby produced fatigue toxins with equal rapidity. A Prl'lu warrior was an excellent sprinter but a poor marathon runner.

As he had expected, the creatures were not following him out of their building. It had cost him a good short spear, cast into the shadows to draw their aim, but he was safe now, in the woods he knew; here even their bizarre weapons would not let the creatures match him.

But his satisfaction was short-lived. The situation at Hrak'un'Mrak was worse than he could ever have imagined it would be. Whatever these blasphemous entities were, they were hostile, and they had struck the first blow. This was a situation not to be tolerated.

The soreness was already leaving him as he stood, and started back up out of the valley, to his brothers.

"That's as far as it will close, Marshal," Biskani said, "One of those shots must have distorted the hinges."

The great slab-like outer door remained wedge at an angle, daylight pouring in through a gap a good two meters wide.

"Wonderful," Rogers said. "That isn't too much of a handicap." He sighed. "All right. I want a fifty percent watch on this chamber at all times. Half the team on full alert right here, the other half ready to come running, four hours on, four off."

"Right," Jefferson said. "I'll take first watch."

"How soon do you think they'll be back?" Biskani asked.

"Just as soon as that fellow can dig up an army," Jefferson said. "I'm sorry, Marshal; but at least we know what happened to Doctor Harris."

"No," Rogers said flatly, "I don't think we do, not yet. Pick your detail, Captain. The rest of the team will fall back into the next chamber and try to rest up."

"Aknol, Marshal."

"I don't see any point in trying to maintain phone silence now. Call me if anything happens."

"Right."

It's weird, Rogers thought, *how just doing something can put you back on the rails again—even if that something isn't really very much. If I had any sense I'd order us back through the doorway right now and seal it off— but I don't feel sensible about this, any more than I believe the Prl'lu got Ruth. So we'll stay, and find her or know why not—but I'm not turning back. Not again.*

"We'll have to find out what other surprises this place is hiding," he said. "I'm going to poke around. The off-watch team can stand down; if I find anything I'll call it in."

"Aknol."

The structure went deep, more than a dozen levels into the ground. There were ramps at opposite ends of each level, obviously intended as substitutes for the massive lift-tubes that stood empty and unpowered at the core of the structure. Rogers descended ramp after ramp. The first two levels, the one they had emerged on and the one beneath it, had held machinery—the great fighting vehicles and rank after rank of sophisticated construction units. Every level below that had been abandoned, holding only long rows of empty stasis cylinders. *This place held the devil's own lot of Prl'lu once,* Rogers thought. *Where did they get to? And why the hell did they leave all that hardware behind?*

The nervousness and tedium of having to explore each level carefully began to frustrate him. He was on the next-to-last level of the Prl'lu complex and there had been no sign of Ruth Harris; for all his earlier certainty he began to wonder if perhaps Jefferson hadn't been right, if perhaps the Prl'lu hadn't taken her when she first emerged from the strange *dis* doorway—or if she had not even left the building on her own. He balked at the last thought. Ruth Harris was a strong-willed woman—all Wilma Deering's female kin seemed to be—and her rashness could match Anthony Roger's own and pull away in a walk, but she was not stupid. If the Prl'lu didn't have her she would be found here, if anyplace. And if she couldn't be found, then the Prl'lu would know how it felt to be hunted. . . .

He descended the ramp to the bottom level—and met himself.

He faced a mirror-smooth surface that blocked the ramp from floor to ceiling. He reached out to touch it, and his fingers slid across its surface as if through air, without the slightest resistance. He pressed straight into its surface, and met resistance, pressure, with no sensation of heat or cold.

He knew what he faced then: a stasis field. And he knew, with sickening certainty, that Ruth Harris was trapped within it. That conviction was at least half self-delusion; it was preferable to assume that she was hidden within a mindless energy field that he could at least hope to control, than to consider that she might instead be in the hands of alien warriors hidden God knew where.

He should have called in his discovery to Jefferson and the crew. That would have been the sensible thing to do. But he was looking for his woman, who was lost because of him, and he was not, ultimately, feeling very reasonable about that. So Rogers set to searching the walls, running his hands over them, looking for controls or seams that might indicate hidden panels or sensors or anything that might let him act. And so he did not notice when the stasis field vanished, and so he never noticed the intricate metal limb that reached out silently behind him until it caught him by the arm and pulled him irresistibly off the ramp. . . .

"You risk much," the Outer Lines Prl'lu said. "You killed our fighting-chief when he demanded that we march on Hrak'un'Mrak. Now you come before us and ask the same thing? How can we accept this?"

"I will say it again," Jak't'rin said, turning as he spoke to include all the warriors ringing him in in his address. "Hrak'un'Mrak is gone, stolen or destroyed by these strangers in their impossible building, who struck at me with weapons of thunder and storm. They have taken the heart of us all and done with it I know not what. I only know that we must challenge them, and demand the Shapers back. We do not march against Hrak'un'Mrak—we march *for* it, and none who are truly of the Blood can refuse. Or would you have the future sons of true warriors curse us as failures and cowards, who refused our duty?"

"Is it truly so clear a choice?" a warrior asked.

"All choices are clear," Jak't'rin answered, "if one sees them clearly. And now you must make *your* choice."

"There is no choice to be made," the first warrior said. He looked around at his companions. "We march for Hrak'un'Mrak. *Ahgn'ki Prl'lu!*"

"*Ahgn'ki Prl'lu!*" a score of voices answered him, as six score had already answered Jak't'rin's call. He would return to Hrak'un'Mrak, to confront its usurpers. And he would not return alone.

The men looked up guiltily as Holcomb and the three troopers entered their barracks. The situation required little guesswork. A floor panel had been pried up and laid aside, and several bundles of dirt lay where they had been dropped, still wrapped in the tunics being used to move them to the toilets.

They must have been at the job for several days; the narrow excavation was already deeper than a man's height. Holcomb looked up from his study of the embryonic tunnel to face the men around him. They wore an assortment of federal and irregular-forces uniforms; he might have served with them not so very long ago.

Now they stared at him with undisguised contempt.

"You're being a little old fashioned about this," Holcomb said. "Wouldn't it have been easier just to dismount one of the *dis* units from the can and use it to tunnel directly?"

"We tried," one of the men said. "They're cast right into the bowls. We couldn't get one loose."

"Ah," Holcomb said. He looked back into the shallow pit. "Fill that in, as best you can. Get that plate back in place. And don't try this again."

"You can't ask that, Holcomb."

"I wasn't asking, soldier," Holcomb said quietly. "That was an order."

"You can't give us an order like that," one man said.

"I'm not going to police our own kind for those bastards!" another shouted.

"Would you rather the Prl'lu did it themselves?" Holcomb asked. "How do you think that would work? How many of our people do you think they'd kill over petty insubordinations or offenses people didn't even know they'd given?"

"I won't serve the Prl'lu," the man said, but not as sharply, this time.

"Then serve the gangs!" Holcomb said. "Like you were supposed to. Protect them—that's our job, isn't it? We did the best we could in the field, now we'll do what we can by staying between the Prl'lu and them. They may end up hating us for it, but at least they'll be alive to hate us. And it has to beat the hell out of tunneling out of the camp when you've got nowhere to go."

He looked around. The men weren't happy, but no one raised a further objection. "Now get that sealed off. We're going to have a lot of work to do, and you'll all be needed."

The conversation had repeated itself with perfect clarity in Shak't'kan's chamber. He had been hard-pressed to restrain his anger when the troopers defied Holcomb; it had amazed him that the human had shown such restraint.

"Plainly, those troops cannot be relied on," he said. "I shall have to order them ended."

"Killed, you mean," Mordred said.

"Of course," Shak't'kan answered him. "I was merely trying to spare your sensitive nature."

Mordred had no trouble at all suppressing his irritation. He had considerably more incentive than the Prl'lu.

"I would advise against killing them," he said. "Such an action would only make Holcomb's task that much harder to complete."

"In what wise?"

"Holcomb has already confronted them over their escape attempt. He did not openly expose them then. If they are suddenly killed now, it will seem as if Major Holcomb is not dealing openly with his men. He will lose their trust, and much of what leverage he still possesses among them.''

"Their respect for Holcomb is not my concern. Order in that camp is.''

"And Holcomb is keeping that order for you. He is saving you wasted troops, wasted time, and wasted lives, as well as preserving for you a useful tool. If you must take action beyond his in this matter, I would counsel you to make Holcomb aware that you know of the attempt, and allow him to suggest a course to take.''

"You believe Holcomb is more capable than I in this?''

"I believe you know how to kill humans superbly well. But you will need Holcomb to learn how to govern them. He is as much a weapon at hand now as a rifle would be in the field. Do not throw a good weapon aside.''

And whatever you do, Mordred thought, *do not destroy those troops. There is nothing else even resembling an organized force on this planet, and without such a force I will be powerless. . . .*

The last redoubt of the Han was not exactly overwhelming in its glory.

The bunkers were sound enough, but they were hand-dug. Open fires were in common evidence, surmounted by mushroomlike 'caps' of woven branches and clay, which Dotty Chan noticed helped to disperse the smoke and perhaps even the heat of the fires, so that each flame would not present a beacon leading hunters to the camp.

The Han were far and away the dominant feature of the camp's population, but Dotty was surprised to notice no small number of the band were white, perhaps twenty out of a hundred, and that they went armed and free among the Han with easy familiarity.

"Are you sure this is a Han camp?" she asked Lu-An, half-seriously.

"It is not the glory that was Lo-Tan, true," the Han woman answered wryly, "but it is what we have made."

"You do keep it simple," the ex-pilot said, watching two small Han men digging at the base of a stump with spades while a bigger, more muscular American wrenched at it with a long pry-bar.

"Of choice, and necessity," Lu-An said. "More complex machinery needs power, which must be stolen or generated, and either practice is liable to detection. Machinery would have to be carried with us. That might slow us down in travel and we cannot risk that; our greatest safety is still in stealth and flight." She smiled. "I should not have to tell an American that—but these were all questions I asked when first they found me, and now I enjoy the chance to seem knowledgeable."

"And what about all these Americans wandering around?"

"Refugees, from fallen gangs. Against the Prl'lu, we have more or less put aside older enmities."

"That must have taken some doing."

"Oh, yes. These Han have been living in the woods since your first War of Liberation. The hostilities ran deep. On the other hand, I *was* the product of a society that taught its women to influence far more sophisticated men than these. I managed to convince them."

"I can imagine. Then you're in charge here."

"In one way or another," Lu-An said, "I don't delude myself into believing that I know more about this life than the men who do the actual running of the camp—but they are men, and easily enough led." She frowned. "In that line, we will have to move now. The demons will be looking for their missing warriors."

"Where will you go?"

"Deeper into the woods. You will forgive me if I am not more specific than that, for now."

"Of course," Dotty said.

"Will you come with us? You would be welcome." Lu-An smiled. "From time to time I do miss reasonably civilized conversation."

Dotty Chan hesitated. "Do you know of any human gangs still loose in these woods?"

Lu-An nodded. "One. Two, perhaps. Actually they are both fragments of a larger gang that was

attacked some weeks ago. But I would not re-
commend joining them. The demons hunt them;
they will be taken soon."

"I have a duty to the gangs, Lu-An."

"Is it a duty you can fulfill successfully?"

"Under the circumstances . . . probably not,
no."

"Then I would suggest that you come with us
for now, and await a better opportunity. There is
no great hurry; the demons will be here for some
time yet, I think."

Dotty Chan looked around herself. The camp
was a simple thing—but it worked, and no one
was hunting them.

"Maybe I will travel with you, for a while."

The first Prl'lu warrior was through the doorway before anyone could even shout.

Jefferson brought the rest of the party rushing
forward as the gate watch opened fire.

Explosions and dis tore at the antechamber of
the Prl'lu base as the tall warriors leaped and
tumbled into the room. Their speed and agility
was beyond belief; the Americans quickly abandoned their dis projectors when they realized
that they were only widening gaps for more warriors to bound through.

A hail of javelins and thrown spears poured
into the doorway. They could not penetrate the
Americans' inertron foil armor, but they struck
with enough force to bruise muscle and break
ribs. The watch at the gate was knocked back-

ward and struck down by the plunging shafts. Then the Prl'lu were in among them with their fighting sticks.

Jefferson halted his detail well back from the melee. There was no point in adding his handful of men and women to that hand-to-hand brawl.

"Aimed fire, single shot!" he ordered. "Independent action! Zero 'em!"

The *Deering* crew threw themselves prone and opened fire. The Prl'lu warriors were quick enough to duck sweeping *dis* beams, but there was no evading concussion and shrapnel.

Two of the gate watch were blown clear of the brawl, to drift lightly through the air on their jump belts. Jefferson detailed two other crew to go after them. The rest continued to pour fire into the faltering Prl'lu. The aliens were courageous beyond question—but they were also intelligent enough to realize that heroism does not always require rushing to a useless death.

"Cease fire!" Jefferson called out. The firing stopped, and with the explosions gone the last movement at the gate had stopped also. Three crew and parts of an indeterminate number of rocket-torn Prl'lu littered the doorway. There was no way to tell how many might lay dead in the antechamber without. Jefferson went forward for his people.

Then the first javelin came arching through the doorway to clatter noisily along the floor. That might even be Prl'lu outside the building entirely; Jefferson could see fresh rays of sunlight where *dis* had gouged openings in the outer walls. Jefferson stepped aside as it skittered past him, then knelt by the body of one of the gate watch. Dead: there was no denying the utility of the Prl'lu fighting sticks. Then he noticed something else.

The crewmember's weapons were gone. . . .

"Damn," Jefferson said softly, then opened his ultrophone-mike. "Marshal, this is Jefferson, up top. The Prl'lu hit our gate watch. We've got three dead and two injured—and we lost four multiplexes to them. Marshal? Can you hear me, Marshal Rogers? Please acknowledge."

The phone stayed silent.

Jefferson swore when it became obvious Rogers could not or would not answer. Then he opened his mike again.

"Everybody, this is Jefferson. We're pulling back into the vehicle area and sealing off the antechamber from inside. Aknol and move."

"Commander," the speaker said, *"we have located the humans who discovered the use of the transit station."*

"Good," Shak't'kan said. "Where are they?"

"Indications are that they have taken the transit point sited on this world's natural satellite. The system is still working."

"Excellent," Shak't'kan said. *Of course,* he thought, *we knew no further installations on this world had fallen. We should have known to look elsewhere.* "Ready a force and prepare to override local control of their transit point. It is time we took it back.''

The storms tore at Talinai unceasingly now, hour after hour, as she staggered through the foothills, no longer thinking of any destination but merely trying to stay alive, and stay in motion, so that the monster Aquintir could not gather another swarm of fiends to overwhelm her. She had lost her last javelin, casting it at a thing with long spidery legs that had followed her for hours, toying with her, always feinting but never quite closing for an attack—until her javelin took it in a careless moment and it died. She had two short spears left, which she carried thrust through her belt, that she might rid herself of their useless quiver, which constantly took on water and weighed her down, or slowed her with repeated stops to empty it. She had lost track of how long this latest assault had been going on, however many hours, however many days. In any real world, she would have collapsed long since of hunger and exhaustion, but those strictures did not apply here. This was a test of mind and will, not of stomach capacity. Her sense of identity and purpose were on trial, and her perceptions of her world; in this lay a clue to possible success, had she not been too fatigued to realize it, had she not already committed her perceptions too firmly to Aquintir's.

A long section of slope was suddenly reduced to liquescent muck and gave way, bearing her down with it. She fought and flailed desperately, and somehow kept her head above the mire, somehow defied the Monster's will that much longer. But it was becoming harder and harder to deny that resistance was useless, when she knew that at a whim Aquintir could have driven those hills together upon her as easily as she might clap her hands.

Yet she fought her way clear of the slide and onto firmer ground, through nothing so much as sheer force of habit. Aquintir would try to kill her, and she would try to live, for as long as the game went on.

She wondered if the Monster was enjoying it.

Talinai lurched and stumbled around the slope of the hill and saw the rocks, with their deep, beckoning shadows. Her memory of Dunlimin's fate was entirely too clear still, but enough was enough. Aquintir could kill her whenever she chose, in whatever manner she chose; Talinai would at least be dry when the blow fell.

She crouched low to crawl beneath the rocks, into the darkness. Several yards in, the passage suddenly opened up enormously, as though some willful gaint had stacked those great boulders to fashion a crude hut. There were gaps, through which air and light reached in, but through tricks of angle and slope and drainage the unceasing storm outside was held at bay.

Talinai drew forth the two spears from her belt, and laid aside her fighting stick, that she might rest more comfortably. And then she looked up and saw the woman staring at her, with the gleaming weapon trained on her heart—

The crewman barely had time to cry out in alarm as the doorway flickered abruptly and Prl'lu warriors stormed through, screaming. He had nothing like enough time to raise the carbine he had reached for before the fire from half a dozen weapons cut him up, down and side-ways.

On the bridge of the *Wilma Deering*, Ordnance Officer Cade had more warning. He heard the crewman's desperate shout and the sudden blast of fire over the intercom channel Rogers had ordered left open between the two posts. He knew that he would be next—but he had time. The Prl'lu would not believe their base could possibly be deserted; they would be bound to search each level and secure it as they moved through the complex.

He left his weapons boards and moved to the main consoles. He closed several switches and the airlock between the *Deering* and the base slammed shut. Then he returned to his own boards. He had no piloting skill, but a certain degree of trim and attitudinal control was necessarily built into the firing systems. He activated his panels and punched in the commands that would align the ship's main batteries on the airlock he had just abandoned.

The great discoid ship eased slowly away from the airlock, clumsy on its relatively weak maneuvering thrusters. The tall, graceful fins that supported the ship's dorsal and ventral ordnance gradually turned to align themselves with the base. Then the *Deering* settled again to rest on the soft lunar soil. Cade sat back, his hands resting lightly on his boards. Now it was up to the Prl'lu.

"Commander, our force has regained control of the lunar transit point."

"Excellent," Hun't'pir said. He felt as much relief as a Prl'lu was capable of feeling. The pirate transit until had been the one real threat remaining to his operations. "What of the humans involved?"

"Our reports indicate that one of them was killed, in the initial assault. The others seem to have retreated to their ship, and have withdrawn roughly one kirr'ek from the base. Their ship shows considerable outer damage, in all probability from their initial attack."

"I would see this ship." He touched his panel and a lunar landscape flickered in before him. The image filled only the forward arc of the chamber; the rest was left flat and opaque, a limitation of such a long-range transmission with relatively crude field equipment. The *Wilma Deering* stood before him, gracefully balanced on its lower pylon, bow on. Even at the normal magnification he was using, Shak't'kan could see places where the ship's unimolecular inertron plates had been blasted away.

"This view was taken by an automatic monitor from just within the outermost lock. Apparently the lock was damaged in the human attack—they had fastened a direct seal between their ship and our base. Up to this point, there have been no responses to our attempts to communicate."

"What action has been taken against the human ship?"

"To now, none. Our base's surface defenses are inoperable. Efforts are under way to dig a tunnel away from the base and send out a flanking party, but that will take time. Our strike force has requested heavier field weapons be sent up for that purpose."

"Do so. But do not attack without my direct orders." The human ship looked to be a surprisingly sophisticated vessel. Presumably the humans who operated it would be of value. "I see no point in gratuitously wasting such a concentration of resources unless necessary. Connect me with the lunar station's transmission channels. We will attempt to negotiate a surrender."

"Yes, Commander."

Cade stared at the speaker in momentary confusion. He had ignored the harsh Prl'lu voices snapping out at him, not comprehending their alien gabble. But this new voice was clearly Prl'lu as well—yet it addressed him in creditable English.

He hesitated. His position was all but hopeless, and he knew it. He could not fly the *Deering* by himself. He had nowhere to go even if he could. With the Prl'lu occupying their base again, there was no way the landing party could return safely, if at all. The *Deering* was not up to a pitched battle—

But there was no way the Prl'lu could know any of that.

He reached over and keyed in screen to go with the harsh voice. A crested, angular Prl'lu face looked out at him.

"I am Shak't'kan, Commander of the Prl'lu forces triumphant upon your Earth. Identify yourself."

"This is the American Alliance Spaceship *Wilma Deering*," Cade answered, "Marshal Anthony Rogers commanding." Well, he would have been. "I am Cade, authorized to attend to communications. What is your message?"

"It is brief. We demand your surrender."

"Our answer is brief. Go to hell. Withdraw your forces from this facility or we will destroy it."

"That is not a viable option on your part."

"As long as we have weapons, it's a viable option."

"You have lost your world. There is no haven

for you, no support. What is left of your government rules at our wish. Surrender."

"What is left of our government is not on the Earth," Cade said. "Marshal Anthony Rogers is the final commander of all Alliance military forces and therefore of the Alliance government for the duration of this crisis. No governmental authority can exceed that."

"Rogers is the commander of a defeated army. We have no need to negotiate with him."

"Then you have no need to talk to me," Cade said, and switched off. He sat back. The odds were against this doing any good—but no other course of action offered him any odds at all. And his bluff accomplished this much: as long as the Prl'lu thought there was a full crew aboard the *Deering*, they might not wonder what other use was being made of the Prl'lu doorway. . . .

Shak't'kan stared at the blank wall before him, frankly bemused by the human's temerity. Then he reopened his microphone.

"Order the officer in charge of our lunar force to send out that flanking party as soon as preparations are made. That ship is now his primary objective."

Rogers remembered the lumbering metal giant and the way it had effortlessly dragged him along, not so much overpowering him as ignoring him, as though any resistance he could possibly offer could not be worth considering. It hadn't even troubled to disarm him, so mindlessly sure was it of its own invulnerability. Rogers certainly wasn't about to disillusion it. Firing off a rocket at such close range was bound to do him more damage than it would his captor.

The sentry robot had pulled him down the long corridor—and into an enormous chamber. Tall ranks of cylinders lined the walls to either side of him, not stasis units but physical tubes of some clear crystal. They were empty, he saw, all but one:

It was obvious that the creature came from the same stock as the Prl'lu. It was tall, taller than a man, but disproportionately slender. But there were differences. The creature in the cylinder had none of a Prl'lu's knobby asymmetry. The joints of the arms and legs were in perfect proportion to those slender limbs, the arachnodactylic fingers correspondingly slim and normally knuckled. Where the Prl'lu had little hair beyond the stiff martial crest above their falconlike faces, this creature had a thick mane above a smooth and expressive face—that betrayed in an instant the madness within it. Rogers could not know of Couilin, or of his collapse under Aquintir's assault, but he could recognize insanity when he saw it. The creature within the cylinder would never leave it in its right mind. Perhaps even the mechanism knew that: as he watched, a slender, telescoping arm descended from the top of the cylinder to pause in front of Couilin's face, where it extruded a tiny extension that carefully placed a drop of some clear solution in each of the open, staring eyes.

The machine pulled him onward. They were coming to the end of the cyclinders now. Rogers noticed that the last few seemed to be occupied. The first one he passed held another of the slender creatures; this one seemed to be sleeping normally—if there was anything normal about this situation. The next creature he passed seemed to be sleeping as well, but its expression hinted at dreams Rogers would not have welcomed.

The next-to-last cylinder held Ruth Harris— and now the machine did immobilize his gun arm as Rogers turned on it with a cry of rage. Three opposed steel digits closed around his forearm with muscle-tearing force; his pistol clattered to the deck beneath him. A smaller extensor snaked out from the metal sentry and picked it up, and the weapon vanished within the machine. The disarming grip shifted to Rogers' upper arm, and he suddenly found himself swung several feet off the floor—and propelled toward the open, empty cylinder before him.

He cursed and kicked backward at the sentry, but his bootheels scored only metal that ignored him. He braced his legs against the far wall of the cylinder and fought back with all his strength, but the machine just kept rolling forward with the same inexorable pressure, forcing him forward steadily until his knees buckled and his feet slipped on the smooth surface of the cylinder, and with a final, abrupt shove he was forced fully within. The tube closed around him with a pneumatic hiss, and he was trapped. He threw his weight against the crystalline barrier, but it paid the impact no more attention than had the metal sentry.

Then he heard the sound, so low as to be almost pure sensation, begin to build. It pierced through him as light would pass through air, with a tingling jolt like a mild electrical shock. Rogers felt his legs begin to grow numb, then his arms, then all feeling fled his body and it stood upright and immobile in the cylinder, answering to commands not his own.

Then the sound began to build within his head, driving his mind back and inward, away from sight, from hearing, from sense itself. Darkness followed the sound, building as it deepened, until finally, at some point he could not determine, the world passed away around him and all was darkness and noise.

He fell.

He did not know to where; he was not even certain that he fell *down*, for all was darkness and he knew he moved only by the floating sensation deep in his gut, like the yawing feeling of an unbalanced belt-jump amplified a hundredfold. His progress could have been endless, or have endured less than an instant.

He began to feel the presences around him: the

presence of the machines, cold and precise and didactic, attempting to communicate with him but failing utterly, their messages reaching him as a liquid, incomprehensible rush of sound. But they continued to try, varying tone and pitch and tempo, seeking the right combination that would let him understand—what?

And he began to feel the second presence then, something dark and somehow solid without substance in the blackness around him, something that seemed to want to expand and encompass everything it met but at the same time walled itself off absolutely, as though afraid to face anything not of itself. The presences interacted, somewhat: he could 'feel' the way the machine presence seemed to hover around the perimeter of the dark thing, poking tentatively at the dark thing but never seeming to unleash its full basso strength, never coming to full grips with it. And he could 'feel' the way the dark thing resisted the machines, striking at their probes with sharp spikes of its dark self. Neither seemed much in the ascendant, but Rogers could not help but feel as though neither of them was unleashing anything like its full power. It was as if they waited on each other for something.

Suddenly, 'ahead' of him in his wild career, Rogers saw that he was about to intersect an aspect of the dark thing, a part of its self put forth and intertwined with the lesser blackness around him. There seemed to be no way he could avoid it; he had no control over his motion.

The blackness flexed elastically as he struck it, and whipped back away from him in a spasm of what might well have been panic. Rogers felt its alarm at this new intrusion thrill through him, and then he was past it.

As though the deeper blackness had been a curtain parting, he suddenly had a destination. Far ahead of himself he could see a tiny pinpoint of white light, distant as a midnight star, alone in the emptiness. Yet even as he watched it, it began to grow, expanding at a rate that spoke of speed beyond calculation. Rogers sincerely hoped that whatever had started him on the wild journey knew how to slow him down again.

The light began to fill the sky ahead of him. Now that he had a reference point his speed was dismaying, a headlong rush that he could not possibly imagine a safe end to. The whiteness was spreading, obscuring everything above and below and to either side of him although he had yet to touch it; he wondered just how vast that radiance was. He was close enough now to make out details—if they were details and not just glare distortions on overstrained retinas; the light seemed to swirl and dance like smoke above a censer, vaporous yet thick as milk.

Then he hit.

He could not help himself—he cried out and flinched as the world around him filled with light and roaring. He had an instant's sensation of wild tumbling, curled into a foetal ball—

—and then it stopped.

Rogers lay huddled for a moment, suddenly aware of a surface beneath him again, waiting for something else to happen. Finally he sat up slowly, and looked around himself.

It was a plain of tortured stone. Great spires of granite had been driven into—no, up out of, he realized, staring at the earth still trapped in nooks and crannies of rock—the moss-covered land around him. And it must have happened fairly recently, too: the soil borne aloft in the spires of rock was still moist and clinging: it had had not yet had time to dry up and blow away.

Rogers got to his feet and scrambled up the nearest spire, looking for his bearings. The plain stretched away into the distance in one direction; to the other, a haze-masked mountain range reared up above the horizon. It was the one definite landmark in sight. Rogers slid down off the spire and started walking.

Aquintir hesitated.

The machines were not attacking her, not anymore—but something was wrong with her world. There were—elements—intruding there, that were not of her creation, and yet they did not challenge her. They merely existed. She did not know if she liked them. She did not know *what* she felt about them, save that they did not try to threaten her as Talinai and the machines had. She sent her feelings out through the world of the tests—all was as she had made it, how she wished it—save for those two discrepancies.

Could they be another trick of the machines, some indirect attempt to act against her in a way they lacked the power and programming to do directly? Even the hesitant anger that question inspired was sufficient to send storm winds shrieking across the broad plains, while clouds gathered and blackened in the skies.

But they *did* nothing. . . .

Less angry than petulant at her confusion, Aquintir withdrew to study this intrusion, to try and make some kind of sense of it. . . .

"Keep your head down," Lu-An said. Dotty pressed lower against the damp earth and crawled forward to where the Han woman lay concealed by a patch of scrub, staring down onto the open ground.

Dis and rocketfire cut and burst through the air above the embattled humans. The Prl'lu squadron swept through again, unhindered, and fire scored the earth in their wake. The six ships arced gracefully into the sky and banked back, in tight formation, contemptuous of the ineffectual groundfire rising to meet them.

"There is nothing we can do to help them," Lu-An said, in reply to Dotty's look. "We have nothing that will match such a force. We should only succeed in getting trapped ourselves."

The groundfire from that trapped gang was lessening a bit more after each fresh Prl'lu attack. Dotty knew what it must be like down there: the noncombatants and wounded crowded into hastily-*dis*ed bunkers; the troops up above fighting back only because there was nothing else to do, knowing their defense was useless, knowing their friends and themselves to be dying for nothing but unable to do anything about it because the Prl'lu were attacking and would continue their attack until it suited them to stop. Had they not been with a gang, the troops could have escaped, easily enough, most of them. They could have scattered, singly and in groups of two or three, offering so many targets that they offered no target at all. But they could not abandon their gang.

The squadron slashed overhead again; again the cycle of attack and lessening retaliation was repeated. But on their next pass, things changed.

With a flare of braking thrusters and repellor rays the Prl'lu squadron eased to a stop above the trapped humans, altering their formation to a six-pointed circle surrounding the gang beneath. Then the barrage began. Fire stabbed down from the Prl'lu ships, which ignored the desperate return volleys of the dying American troops as they methodically walked their salvos across the human positions After five minutes, nothing returned their fire from below; after ten, nothing that still lived above ground was moving to advertise that fact.

Then Dotty saw the gleam along the horizon as the transports were called in, two of them, great bulbous ships that trundled forward driven by enormous lifting fans.

The transports settled slowly to the ground beyond the perimeter defined by the hovering warships. Ramps, ridiculously small against the bulk of the hulls that emitted them, lowered to the ground and troops began to emerge, fanning out in graceful, jump-belted arcs. Lu-An turned to the Han at her other side. "Order the others to withdraw deeper into the woods. Slowly; we don't want to draw attention to ourselves now."

Lu-An and Dotty pressed even lower behind their cover as one detachment of the Prl'lu force came bounding into position not a hundred yards from their hiding place. And Dotty felt her stomach twist.

Few Prl'lu had bright yellow hair, or wore what were obviously Alliance military coveralls overlaid with a dun, surplice-like garment. The troops she watched were human, and the masters they so clearly served were Prl'lu.

Stunned and disbelieving, she watched the captured gang being herded out of its bunkers and aboard the transports by their human wardens. It didn't take very long.

Lu-An looked over and saw that Dotty Chan had dug her fingers deep into the soil before her.

"Still want to try and go back?" she asked.

"I don't believe it," Dotty said, "I *can't* believe it. Those were humans, federal troops, and they were *with* Prl'lu!"

"It's not surprising," Lu-An said, "that's probably the only way that your government could retain any power at all. It might even be for the best. I remember what it was like when our city faced the Prl'lu directly; your own people can't be any worse."

Dotty didn't speak.

"But if you go back now," Lu-An said, "you'll probably wind up doing just what they did. You're still an Alliance officer."

"I couldn't do that. I'd refuse."

"The Prl'lu do not cope well with refusal."

"I . . . I still couldn't. I won't." She looked away from the field, where the transports were lifting off. "Do you folks have room for one more?"

Holcomb sat apart from his men in the belly of the enormous transport, sick with self-loathing.

He had repeated all his own arguments to himself, all the arguments he and Mordred had used on each other. It was better that the Alliance troops stay between the gangs and the Prl'lu, it had to be. It was safer for the gangs, to avoid direct contact between them and the Prl'lu. And it was better for the future, because it left the humans an organized structure of their own, not entirely under Prl'lu control—however limited it might be, such a structure would be necessary to defend human interests in the future. And it had saved the lives of many of Holcomb's troops, for whom the Prl'lu might have found little use otherwise. They were good arguments, well thought out and rational.

And they none of them amounted to a hill of

beans beside the look in the eyes of the people they had herded out of those bunkers, who had seen sons and daughters, lovers and parents, murdered by inhuman monsters—and had then seen humans in the uniforms they had counted on for protection working under those same aliens. He might save his people from the Prl'lu, he thought, but now he had irrevocably denied himself any place among them.

CHAPTER SIX

"Get that hatch open!" Jefferson shouted. Then he threw himself down as the *dis* beam slashed through the wall behind him again.

He rolled to his feet and ran, as weapons blazed from the parked vehicles ahead of him, covering his retreat. He leaped for the track-guard of the nearest machine—and something struck him a stunning blow in the back. It must have been a javelin, or perhaps a short throwing spear, for his foil armor stopped the blow and the impact did not kill him.

At least not at once. The blow drove his wind from him and set him tumbling, and the secondary impact as he slammed against the track-guard and rebounded all but knocked him sense-less. He started to slide back off the track-guard—and Peggy Biskani caught him, leaning far out of the open personnel hatch to snare his boot and hold on. If they hadn't both been wearing jump belts, neither would have avoided fall-ing.

Biskani heaved, pulling Jefferson up until he could grasp the sill of the hatchway. Other hands caught at him then, and pulled him in.

He forced himself upright as the hatch was slammed shut and dogged down, and moved to the vision slit. Here and there he could see figures scurrying across the far end of the hallway, taller than men, while swathes of *dis* cut away the anteroom doors from outside. The Prl'lu primitives were putting their captured arms to good effect. They were safe, for the moment, he thought; the Prl'lu were unlikely to build such a massive fighting machine without taking the obvious precaution of protecting it against *dis*.

But the Prl'lu would be in among the great machines in moments, and then they would be trapped where they were.

Well, at least there were worse places to be trapped than in a heavily armed fighting machine.

He turned to Biskani. "See if this thing has any power available, and see whether you can at least get a couple of the turrets operational."

"Right." She popped the inside hatch to the crowded personnel lack and moved off into the machine. Jefferson moved back to the vision slit and watched their outer barricades going down.

Jak't'rin cried out triumphantly as the pale light from the foreign weapon slashed at the great stone building, cutting through it as easily as his spear cut air. The power of the weapon excited him. He had found a way to make it spit flaming darts that burst like thunder and rent great pits in earth and stone, and now he had learned to make it do *this*. Surely even the Shapers could not provide greater wonders!

The other warriors bearing the captured weapons listened to his shouted revelation, and added their fire to his. Gate and lintels crumbled and vanished, and the gathered of the Blood rushed forward in a body, to confront their enemies in triumph. . . .

Then something gigantic and gleaming surged through the shattered doorway, and Jak't'rin's host scattered before it. Spears and javelins clattered off shining metal as they fell back; the enormous bands of linked blocks that it rode on gouged deep furrows in the earth.

Jak't'rin turned the blue light of his new weapon upon the machine, and was stunned to see it lumber forward as if nothing was amiss. He changed his grip on the weapon, and hurled his flaming darts against the monster. Fire and noise wreathed it, but it never slowed—and now smaller structures atop it were swivelling, and lowering long tubes to point into the warriors swarming around it. Fire and thunder burst now amid their ranks, and many died as they fled.

The weapon went silent in Jak't'rin's hands. No more flaming darts leaped from it; he had exhausted them. He could only watch, perplexed, as the largest structure atop the machine turned to face back into the building it had abandoned—and that building erupted in flame.

Then, to his horror, he recognized the machine. Surely it was one of those he had seen on his long-ago pilgrimage to Hrak'un'Mrak, or one so like them as to be of common origin. Doubt suddenly assailed him, all the more urgently for its irremediable nature.

What if that vast structure was in fact Hrak'un'Mrak itself, transfigured by some process and for some reason beyond his comprehension? What if—though he almost failed and conceiving the thought, so great was his horror—the strange beings they had assailed were in fact the Place of Awakening's natural masters? What if, in hopes of keeping an ancient trust, he had violated it absolutely, committed the grossest sacrilege?

What if he raised his hand against the Shapers themselves, and had slain his masters?

He turned to the warriors surrounding him, casting aside his weapon, the instrument of his blasphemy.

"Run!" he ordered them. "Regroup the warriors! Order them to withdraw at once, and cease all attacks!" He saw the uncomprehending looks of the other bearers of the captured weapons, and their hesitation flayed him. "We may be guilty of blackest sin!" he cried. "Now run!"

Slowly at first, but urged on by his obvious conviction, the warriors turned and vanished into the woods. Jak't'rin turned and looked down on the machine, now sitting silent and invincible in the field before the ravaged structure, and wondered how completely he had damned himself.

"We're out," Jefferson called.

"Did I miss the wall?" Biskani's voice came back through the earphones of his helmet.

"There wasn't any wall left to miss. Think you can stop this thing?"

"Hell, I'm surprised I got it started. I think so. Hold on." There was a sudden lurch and the machine jerked to a halt. *"Close enough. Look at them scatter."*

"Maybe that's the secret to dealing with a Prl'lu. All you have to do is outweigh 'em by a few thousand tons," Jefferson said. "Have we got power to the turrets?"

"I pushed enough buttons. Something must have happened."

"Let's give it a try." Jefferson pushed down on the right-hand pedal by his seat in the small secondary turret. There was a brief whine of motors and a click; the turret trembled but didn't move. He cursed, then realized that the traversing mechanism would have to have a governor system to prevent it from turning into the vehicle's hull. He stamped the leftward pedal and the turret spun smoothly in that direction. He leaned forward on the grips set in the panel before him, and the bulky mechanism of the gun beside him canted upward, lowering the muzzle.

There was no question what the stud on the right-hand grip was for. The gun began to crack out rounds. Even with the external pickups of his helmet cut out, the reports were deafening.

"Jefferson to all batteries," he called, "the pedals are for traverse, the grips for elevation. Hit 'em."

Within seconds, the field around the fighting machine was clear of living Prl'lu.

"What now, Captain?" Biskani's voice came up to him.

"Let's see if we can get the primary turret armed," he answered. "We figured out how to drive this one; I'd hate to see some genius out there repeat the trick."

"But Marshal Rogers is still missing inside the complex."

"I know that; we'll have to risk it. I want those vehicles unavailable to these people. The Marshal is on his own now."

The mountains loomed far higher now, only exaggerating the isolation of the lone human figure trudging toward them across the plain.

Ruth Harris started at the slender figure curled up around itself across the cave. The being had stared at her for a long moment three days ago, when first it crawled into the cave out of the storm. Then it had simply lain itself down, as though certain she would not kill it, and apparently went to sleep.

Since that time it had virtually ignored her; it did not react to her questions, it ignored her attempts to communicate by gesture—the only time she had got a rise out of it was when she had screamed at the top of her lungs and dashed a fist-sized rock against the wall above its head. It had actually flinched, that time: small reward for a sore arm and raw throat.

Talinai felt little urge to leave the shelter of the cave. It was well-lit and airy, yet quite secure from the elements—and Aquintir had shown no interest in attacking her there. Even the strange creature across from her was no disturbance, once Talinai knew she could discount it as a threat. She ignored its attempts to communicate: she didn't know what aspect of Aquintir's world the creature was meant to represent but there could scarcely be any point in conversing with one of the Monster's creations.

And it was so easy just to relax, just to lay there and let the world go by, undisturbed and undisturbing. What it came down to was that Talinai had very little desire left to continue exerting herself in a test she had no hope of winning, not when it was easier still just to lay back and let whatever happened, happen. Considering her dismal failure so far, it had to be as good a course of action as any other.

The day continued peaceful. The sun shone in—which sun? Ruth wondered—through the natural vents in the cave. All was quiet as the Earthwoman and the beaten Shaper stared at each other.

*   *   *

Cade watched the tunnel's progress unhappily. Several kilometers' distance and several meters' worth of sterile lunar soil overhead must have seemed like good camouflage—but it was hard to hide anything from an ultroscopic scanner.

The question was, what should he do about it? He knew what it had to be, of course—a flanking action, an attempt to get forces into the field against the *Deering* without suffering the punishing casualties of a full frontal assault directly into her massed batteries. Prl'lu were brave, not suicidal. But should he let them continue their tunnel, or should he move against it now?

Prudence won out. *Dis* gave a tunneling team too much latitude. They could pop their bore up into the open at any time it suited them; there was no sense in giving them their chance.

He booted his board up off standby and keyed in instructions. A secondary missile battery swung to aim its tubes off toward the horizon. Targeting figures were locked in, for fixed points along the tunnel, and one sight with a gap left for his estimate of the tunneling unit's progress.

He fired.

A string of explosions erupted a kilometer apart as the missles impacted along the tunnel's course. The final warhead erupted with particular vigor: Cade assumed that had been the added energy of the tunneling team's *dis* power packs going up. He sat back and reached for the microphone switch, to upbraid his opponents—

—alarms shrilled in the cabin. Too late, he saw the pinpoint telltales of half a dozen objects approaching the *Deering*, from a point well short of his first missile's impact. Another advantage of *dis*, he suddenly realized: you didn't have to open a tunnel only at the ends. . . .

He leaned into his boards again and tapped out commands. His secondary missile and *dis* batteries swerved to lock on the new threat. Fire went out. He watched as the Prl'lu missiles tried to evade his counterfire, but nevertheless winked out one after the other. As two of his missiles began to close in on the last one, he relaxed—

—and the *Deering* lurched savagely, almost before the new alarms. He looked back and saw a numbing sight on his forward screens.

It looked like racks of panpipes, four high, rising up out of the ruined airlock of the base on its supporting floater as Prl'lu swarmed out over the lunar landscape. As he watched, bright quicknesses leaped from two more of its tubes as the *Deering* staggered again, the mobile launcher drifting off-camera as the ship heeled off its landing gear and began a slow topple in the lunar gravity.

Cade punched for trim and thrusters through the battery alignment systems. The *Deering* halted its downward slide, gouts of the lunar dust rolling away across the landscape. The ship rolled upright again, and pivoted, and the full salvo the Prl'lu launched struck into the ship, targeted on the primary ordnance fins. Cade cursed as system after system died before him. He went to the secondary batteries, swinging them around from their flanking lines of fire, but the Prl'lu infantry were firing now, with shoulder-launched weapons that hurtled in from all directions, knocking out *dis* beams and lesser missile racks and rocket cannon. In seconds there was not an operable battery on the ship, and Cade could hear the first metallic footsteps as boarders landed on the outer hull.

He had one weapon left.

He keyed in maneuvering thrusters. Slowly, but with steadily increasing momentum, the *Wilma Deering* canted forward and slid toward the Prl'lu base. Cade could see the vacuum-armored infantry ahead of the ship leaping aside as they fired off their weapons; the *Deering* shuddered and lurched at each fresh wound, but she continued to advance.

Cade cut the thrusters. Coasting freely now, the *Wilma Deering* began to settle along her bal-listic arc—and rammed squarely into the Prl'lu base. The damaged airlock was ruptured en-tirely: deep within the base heavy airlock doors bisected corridors as those Prl'lu fortunate enough to be in or near vacuum armor struggled to don it—and those that weren't died.

The full weight of the crippled ship fell against the base. Its outer shell already breached and weakened, the *Deering* drove cleanly through, crushing first one level, then a second, then a third. The Prl'lu on those levels were fortunate; at least they died quickly.

Wreathed in rubble and expanding gas, the *Wilma Deering* halted, half its length driven into the base. Cade pushed away from his boards, as puncture alarms and damage klaxons shrilled and honked around him. The boards around him—those that still worked, at least—told the full story: without vacuum armor, there was no place in the ship beyond the bridge that he could survive for more than seconds.

So. He wondered if the time he had bought for Rogers and the others had done any good. There was no way to tell, of course, not now. But it had done this much, that he knew: Ordnance Officer Cade had messed up more Prl'lu than anyone could have expected him to. He'd have to settle for that, he imagined.

When the hatchway blew and the second Prl'lu stepped over the body of the first, the warrior was surprised to note that the dead human who had gunned down his predecessor hadn't even bothered to get up from his chair to do it. . . .

"They must be found," Shak't'kan said. "Initiate a search through every transit point, and do not cease until they have been found."

His dispassionate voice betrayed little of the Prl'lu commander's cold fury. The humans had shown courage in the past, and commendable fighting skill, in perspective—but they had never outthought the Prl'lu, outmaneuvered them.

Except that now they had. An undetermined number of humans, sophisticated enough to understand the operation of the transit system, at loose somewhere within it . . . they could not win, of course. But they could do untold damage.

And the worst of it was, they might never know where the humans had gone, until it was too late. It was one thing to give an order, 'find them'; but the possibility of it was a different matter. If the humans had not maintained the transit point from both ends, but only from the lunar base, with the receiving station slaved in, then they were gone without a trace, until they reactivated the system from wherever they were. Until then, there was nothing they could do about the humans. . . . *damn* that Cade-human! He had acted better than Shak't'kan would have believed possible. He wondered how many more of the humans in his keeping would be as likely to refuse to surrender. . . .

"Chan, what's wrong?" Lu-An asked.

"Oh, nothing much," Dotty Chan said. "I've only watched people I was supposed to protect being herded like cattle. I've only seen my own people herding them . . ." she sighed. "I don't think I can stay here, Lu-An."

"Why not? You're fitting in well enough. It's only been a few days—"

"It's not that," Dotty said. "Do you remember when you asked me if I could fulfill my responsibility to the Alliance? Well, I think it's become necessary that I try."

"And how will you try? What do you think you can do against the demons?"

"Against the Prl'lu? Nothing, I suppose. But against their servants . . . maybe I can do something. I think I have to try, at any rate."

"You don't sound very convinced of that."

"I'm not convinced of it. I'm scared sick of it. But I think it's something I'm going to have to do."

"You mean to go after the humans you saw aiding the Prl'lu."

Dotty Chan nodded. "They have to have a leader. They have to have someone who organized them for the Prl'lu."

"You'll kill him, then?"

"If I can reach him. It shouldn't be impossible."

"If you can find him, if they'll take you in, if you wind up close enough to him, no, it shouldn't be. But that's an unlikely list of conditions."

"Yes, it is, isn't it?"

"I'm not talking you out of this, am I?"

"I wish to hell you could."

Lu-An sighed. "I cannot help you in this. I cannot risk these people. Their lives are already perilous enough."

"I understand. This isn't something they could help with anyway."

"I can let you have food and equipment; I can
do that much."

"I appreciate it."

"You're killing yourself."

"Odds are."

She left the next morning, shouldering her
pack and belting easily off to the west. Few of
them watched her go.

It had proven harder to convince the gathered
warriors to stop their attacks than it had been to
get them to join him in the first place. But when
Jak't'rin explained what he feared they had done,
they were only too happy to let him assume the
full weight of the blame, as well as the duty of
making pilgrimage to the shrine they had half-
demolished in search of the truth.

He stood at the edge of the woods facing
Hrak'un'Mrak. The great war machine still rested before the ruined gate, its mighty weapons
trained on the woods. The sun was setting across
the valley; when it finally fell below the line of
the encircling ridge he would go, and trust to the
darkness to spirit him past the enormous guardian. And if it didn't, then perhaps that might be a
judgement all its own. . . .

Talinai tried to ignore the howling in the distance. She didn't want to hear it, didn't want to
believe she *was* hearing it. She wasn't *doing* anything, why wouldn't Aquintir leave her alone?

Ruth had reached for her pistol at the first caterwaul from over the hill. The way Talinai cowered before the noise only emphasized the undeniable evil she had heard in that sound.

Ruth crawled to the mouth of their cave and looked out. The slopes before her were clear, but the howling she heard was louder now, drawing closer. And then she heard something else: bellowed human cursing, frightened and angry.

She was sliding down the slope and running toward the noise before she could think about it.

Talinai watched the creature leave the cave. She felt no urge to follow it, no desire to face the Monster's swarm yet again—but suddenly the cave seemed a lonely, cramped place, no longer sheltering but confining, someplace where she could be trapped, and penned up, perhaps even locked in. . . .

She decided to follow the creature. If nothing else, perhaps she could keep it from doing something foolish.

Talinai caught up with Ruth as she crested a low rise. The howling was almost a tangible thing on the other side of it. Together they scrambled over the top, to look down at the milling horror—

"Tony!" the creature beside her screamed. Talinai checked the reflexive swing of her fighting stick barely in time. Ultimate horror made her nervous, but it didn't bother her nearly as much as what Ruth Harris saw bothered her:

Rogers had got his back to an overhang, and

was clubbing at the gibbering impossibilities that swarmed up the slope toward him with a spike of stone. It was not much of a weapon; although the comparatively steep slope he had climbed hampered the larger, more formidable beasts somewhat, so that he had faced only the smaller, quicker ones so far, he was already bleeding from half a dozen deep cuts and gashes.

Talinai felt pity for the creature. It was fighting bravely, but it would not survive much longer—

—there was a shrill, whistling sound from beside her, and fire blossomed among the creatures below them. Talinai turned and saw the creature she had followed with its weapon out. Thin streams of fire and smoke were leaping from its muzzle, to explode with savage force among the beasts in the gully. Talinai was reminded of slaughtered Pehr, and his gleaming weapons.

Rogers looked up as the rocketfire scattered his assailants.

"Ruth!" he shouted.

"Get up here, Tony, fast!" Ruth Harris shouted back.

Rogers scrambled out from beneath his overhang, careful to avoid her line of fire, and scrambled up the slope toward them. The field before them had been swept clear of living things: the swarm had withdrawn into the broken cover, out of Ruth's line of fire.

"That was one hell of a welcoming party," Rogers said, as Ruth ripped up what was left of his tunic to try and stay the bleeding from several of the deeper cuts on his shoulders and back. "I think I owe you, lady."

"Nothing like that for me," she agreed. "How did you get here, Tony?"

"Those tubes, behind the stasis field. That's the last I remember, after that damned tin man caught hold of me. The same for you, I suppose—ouch."

"Pretty much," she agreed. Her voice was bleak. "I'm sorry I got you into this, Tony. But we just couldn't leave the Prl'lu doorway alone—I couldn't, anyway. It seemed like the only shot we had left."

"It probably was," Rogers agreed. "You saw the base we found there."

"Mm-hmm. Where was it when we needed it?"

"Right there. And we can still use it—if Jefferson can hang on to it."

"Jefferson's still back at the Prl'lu base? You brought the crew through?"

"Most of them. I just hope they're enough."

"Why shouldn't they be? That base was deserted."

"Not when we got there." He told her the story as far as he knew it, up to Jak't'rin's first encounter with the humans.

Ruth Harris was skeptical. "Machines like we found there—and a Prl'lu was throwing spears at you?"

"Uh-huh. What's your informed opinion of that?"

"I haven't got one. It doesn't make any sense."

"I was afraid you'd say something like that," Rogers said. "Moving on to more immediate concerns, have you got any idea where are now?"

"Ah," Ruth said. "Now this I know you're not going to like."

"Uh-oh," Rogers said, sitting up stiffly. The bleeding was not entirely checked yet, but the pressure of the bandages felt good. "When a *Deering* woman gets nervous, it's time to panic. What's your theory, Doctor?"

"I think we're still in the tubes, Tony."

Rogers stared at her. "No."

"I think that's the case. Look at that creature over there, Tony." She pointed to the silent Talinai, back in her corner. "Do you recognize it?"

"Not especially."

"I think she was in the tube next to mine when that robot was locking me in. In fact, the more I look at her, the more certain I am of it."

"That's not much in the way of evidence."

"There's more. When was the last time you felt hungry or thirsty?"

"I can't remember. Scared, I remember, but not hungry."

"I haven't wanted anything to eat since I arrived here, Tony, and subjectively that's been a good four days. Maybe nerves could kill my appetite, but I haven't been thirsty, either, and that's just not possible. And you want one more piece of evidence?"

"Go ahead."

"How many shots did I fire before?"

"I wasn't exactly counting," Rogers said. "But you did chew them up pretty good."

"Tony, I must have fired fifty rounds back there."

"And—?"

"I only have the one ten-shot magazine load."

"Hmm."

"You want to see something else interesting?" she passed him the handgun. "According to the magazine indicator, I have still have ten rounds left."

"That's unreal."

"Exactly."

"You mean I'm dreaming this?"

"You are, or I am, or somebody is—and we're sharing it, somehow." She grinned. "I wonder how you'd look with a beard."

"Forget it," Rogers said, half-expecting his face to start to twitch with hyperactive bristles.

"Relax, Tony, I don't think it works that way. If it did, I'd have dreamed my way awake by now; I've tried. Whatever's going on, it isn't an entirely random situation. Something is controlling it."

"How?"

"If I knew that. . . ."

"Yeah. I wonder if there's a way out of this."

"I haven't found one."

"Well, there has to be one."

"Why?"

"Because this is one hell of an inefficient way to keep prisoners. So it's not a jail. All we have to do now is figure out what it is and how to get out of it."

"Oh, is that all?" Ruth said.

Rogers grinned. "It should kill a few minutes."

"Or us," Ruth said. "But there's no way around that now. In the meantime, you lay down and give those cuts a chance to clot."

Rogers eyed the sandy floor of the cave sourly. "What about infection?"

"It's up to you. Personally, if I'm not going to get hungry I refuse to fester."

"Yeah, I suppose." Rogers stretched out stiffly, on his stomach. "Wake me in an hour."

"No. You sleep as long as you feel like. We'll do whatever we do next when we have to. Doctor's orders."

"The doctor is a physicist."

"And you're very physical. Now get some rest. God knows when you'll get the chance again."

Aquintir was frightened.

The anomalies had resisted her. She had sent forth her horrors against Talinai again, to torment her and perhaps even slay her this time, and grant her release from her awareness of Aquintir's superiority. She had known that the swarms would pass the one anomaly, and that the other rested near Talinai, but she had never meant to attack either of them.

But the first oddity had actually attacked the foremost of the swarm itself, when they drew near—and the second had slaughtered them in drove. Worse, it had usurped a part of her own power to do so, striking at them with a weapon that seemed incapable of exhausting itself—for it wasn't, not as long as the anomaly wanted it to continue firing.

She would have to destroy them, now. She could tolerate a mystery, or at least shut it out, but she could brook no opposition—and certainly no usurpation of her prerogative of control.

The stones began to tremble. Rogers sat up abruptly as the ground shook under him and dust sifted down from between the leaning rocks.

"Aquintir!" Talinai screamed. Rogers and Ruth Harris stared as the Shaper threw itself past them and out the crawlway. The rocks lurched again. They wasted little time in following.

Outside, a bizarre sight met their eyes. The foothills were rippling like water. Where ridges had crested, arroyos widened and deepened as they watched. A spire of stone settled back into the ground like the prow of a sinking ship, then surged upward again, almost breaking free of the soil entirely before it pitched over to impact thunderously upon the ground. Boulders the size of their heads were bouncing wildly about, like grains of sand shaken from a blanket. In the distance the mountains themselves seemed to be bearing down on them like icebergs into a bay.

Talinai was still running, as well as she could in that lurching terrain. She stumbled, and fell, and staggered upright and ran and fell and struggled to her feet and ran again, as Couilin had run out on the plains.

Rogers and Harris looked after her, then felt the ground beneath their feet begin to move. They turned.

The hillock behind them was driving forward like the prow of a ship, casting aside a wake of scattered earth.

"This can't be happening!" Rogers shouted. He'd worked in mines; he thought he knew all the ways stone and earth under pressure could behave—and this was none of them.

"Tell it that when it gets here," Ruth answered him. They joined Talinai in her outward flight.

The hills convulsed around them, buckling and writhing as though they hoped to catch the fleeing humans in a great stone fist. They didn't so much run as squirm over the twisting land, always seeking the highest ground, always abandoning it for the next temporary peak as it yielded beneath them. They spent as much time on their bellies as on their feet, as much time sliding helplessly as they did climbing or running, and if either of them helped the other more, supported the other more than he or she supported themselves, they were never able to sort it out afterward.

The convulsions refused to stop. Looking back, Rogers could see that what had seemed to be an illusion before was cold fact—the distant mountains were moving, lumbering forward. Already they stood out, clearly distinct, stripped of their distance-haze. They must have been covering miles to show that kind of change. That wasn't something they could fight. Blindly, with as little sense of destination as the half-crazed Shaper they followed, they fled across the rippling plains.

Prudence had won out over guilt. In the end Jak't'rin had not abandoned his skills so rashly as to rush across an open field in view of the enormous war machine guarding Hrak'un'Mrak. Instead he had circled around behind the building, putting its mass between the sentinel and his approach. Edging along the walls and through the abandoned gateway had been a much simpler matter.

He was appalled by the destruction he found within. One or two of the distant lighting panels overhead were still operable, by them he could see crumbled stone and twisted metal all across the chamber. How much had he and the tribesmen done, he wondered, and how much was from the one mighty salvo of the guardian machine? Could they have destroyed their own wealth as a punishment for the rebellious Blood, that they might never know the glory of such mighty arms?

He moved through the dark halls, between rows of fighting machines. This far back, the machines seemed whole in the half-light, huge asymetrical silhouettes that hemmed him in on all sides.

He reached the far wall of the vehicle chamber. Wide tubes opened before him, descending into the depths of the structure. With no idea how to use them, he was forced to turn aside, and at length he discovered the ramp.

He followed them down into history, past the levels of empty stasis cylinders that had contained his fathers until their time of awakening, when it became their task to set out into the world and ready it for the Shapers who had never followed. *And now never might*—he broke off that thought.

He reached the bottom of the rampway. A shining surface of gleaming mirror-brightness faced him. His heart quickened. It was just such a gleaming surface that Hrak'un'Mrak had once presented to the outside world, breached only briefly and in part for the pilgrimages of the fighting-chiefs. Jak't'rin had descended as far as he could on his own. With such patience as he could muster, he set aside his weapons and seated himself before the impassable barrier, prepared to wait for however long it took.

When the barrier dissolved away and the metal guardian slid forward to tower over him, he stood and took up his weapons, and followed it willingly.

Confusion and relief warred within his mind as he stared at the cylinders and their mixed contents.

"Then I have not blasphemed?" he asked, hardly daring to hope. . . .

"*Anomalous influences have penetrated the facility,*" the guardian replied, in a voice like spearheads and wire. "*In conjunction with sub-optimal testing output, circumstances justify exceptional system response.*"

It was as close to an absolution as Jak't'rin would ever receive.

He stepped forward, looking around himself. "Why do the Shapers not awake? Why have you lain these intruders in beside them?"

"*Suboptimal testing output justifies exceptional system response.*"

"But why the intruders? Why this—exceptional system response?" Maybe if he spoke its language, the machine would begin to make sense.

"*Distortion of the test matrix beyond system modification and correction options indicated insertion of randomizing elements.*"

"What test do you speak of?" Jak't'rin asked.

"*Shaper selective and hierarchical alignment testing.*"

"Shaper—? Is this where the Shapers are born?"

"*Organic generation and conditioning not a function of this system.*"

"Then what is your function?" Jak't'rin asked, in rising impatience.

"*This system assesses optimum perceptive, attitudinal and psychological fitness.*"

That was so much gibberish to the spear-carrying warrior.

"Why?" he asked.

"*The Shapers must be fit to rule,*" the machine said, making the one sensible statement it had spoken so far.

"Then you try them? As the land tries Prl'an and Blood?"

"*That analogy achieves a high level of congruence.*"

"When will they awaken?"

"*Revival not possible under distorted test matrix.*"

"The trial is flawed?"

"*Yes.*"

"How?"

"*Overinvolvement of the primary test subject has led to perceptive, attitudinal and psychological impairment. Impaired subject has engendered corporal disfunction among subsequent subjects.*"

"What does that mean?" Jak't'rin asked.

"*One hundred and four subsequent subjects have exhibited terminal vital functions.*"

"The Shapers are dying?"

"*Yes.*"

Jak't'rin turned to look at the long column of empty cylinders once again, horror-stricken by what they now implied. "You must stop that!"

The machine's voice could not change.

"Distortion of the test matrix extends beyond system modification and correction options."

"Is there nothing you can do?"

"Insertion of randomizing elements shows little effect to date."

"Then you cannot save them?"

"No."

Jak't'rin looked at the empty cylinders, turned back to the impassive machine.

"Then what can I do?"

"Inappropriate query. Querying unit is a Prl'lu/Protector. Systems respond to Prl'arek/ Shaper parameters."

"Yes!" Jak't'rin shouted. "I am of the Blood! I am Prl'lu, of the Protectors! And I must protect the Shapers! How can I do that here?"

"Corporal integrity of test subjects is this system's function—"

"You have failed at your function!" Jak't'rin accused. "The Shapers die, they are impaired, they exhibit terminal vital functions or whatever you want to call it! But they must be protected! As long as one Shaper lives, you must protect it —I must protect it! Tell me *how!*"

The metal sentinel seemed to hesitate. Then the voice rolled out again, ringing and impassive as ever.

"A valid scenario exists for further randomiz-

ing input," the machine said.

"Does that mean you'll tell me how to—" and then he cried out at the pressure as the sentinel's great metal hands clamped down on his arms. The machine swung him up from the floor, as easily as it might have wielded a human. The numbing current was coursing through his body before the cylinder had even finished closing.

Darkness crept over him—and knowledge burst into his mind like a spike of solid light. Even as he plummeted downward on the eternal/instantaneous journey into the machine's scenario, the testing systems filled him with the knowledge he would need to understand the experience, and to survive long enough to deal with it.

Jak't'rin was awestruck by the immensity of the process he had immersed himself in. He had guessed rightly when he asked the machines if this 'test' was to the Shapers what taming the world had been to the Prl'lu and the Prl'an, but he had not imagined the half of it.

The Prl'lu were the Prl'arek, the Shapers—as much as the Prl'an were the Prl'lu and the reverse. All came from the same base stock; none was born more or less one or the other, except as the chance pairing of chromosomes indicated.

Why had he not seen that before? he wondered. He had been a fighting-chief; he had participated in the selections of the village young himself, and had overseen the managing of diet and schooling and conditioning that had turned stocky farmers' infants into long-limbed warriors. He should have seen what that implied, what the possibility of that implied. He hadn't, of course. That was part of the conditioning as well: the pride, the sense of superiority a warrior needed. Even if that warrior was nothing more than a farmer who reaped death instead of grain.

Where had that thought come from? He had been more than willing to admit his fallibility as a warrior; you could not know pride of accomplishment, take satisfaction in true service, if you did not know fear of failure, however deeply buried. But he had never, could not, feel condescension toward his role.

And then he identified it. It was the teaching of the Prl'arek, to whom the Prl'lu were as much servants as the Prl'an were servant to the Prl'lu. It was how one had to consider *everything* to be a true Shaper; it all had to be considered in terms of utility, of usable resource. Prl'an, Prl'lu . . . even Prl'arek. Even one's self.

He was chilled by the isolation and loneliness of such a philosophy. A Prl'lu, at least, could feel the satisfaction of duty well performed; even a Prl'an could know the gratification of a task finished. But the Prl'arek could not—their duty never ended, not as long as there was a system to be maintained.

And the scale of the systems they maintained astonished him. He had been awed by the glory of shaping an entire world—two worlds, actually, he noted absently, and knew that there were in truth those of the Blood on the distant blue star he had stared at so often, and that they awaited the coming of the Shapers as ardently as he had. But that was the least, tiniest, insignificant part of the system the Shapers ruled in the name of the three races. . . .

More immediately useful knowledge came to him, then. He learned of the madness of Aquintir, and how she had intertwined herself with the reality of the test, perverting it to her insane fantasy of supremacy. He witnessed the piecemeal slaughter of the Prl'arek, while the machines tried to cope with the contradiction of Shapers dying in the test when the testing system was forbidden to kill Shapers. The contradiction was slowly destroying the system, he noticed—otherwise it would never have tried such desperate, unlikely therapies as inserting the intruders or even Jak't'rin himself into the system as palliatives.

And he saw how Aquintir had made herself strong, and how the others had died. First into the system, she had made its conceptual reality her own, and when the others had challenged her, they had made the fatal error of challenging her in her own context. They had then died, for no creature will dream up a delusion that does not go exactly as it wishes it to go.

He would not make that mistake, he decided. He was Prl'lu and there was nothing else that mattered. It was *his* reality that Prl'lu defended their charges, and did not fall. He had faced the spikeslinger, he faced others of the Blood—now he would face insanity, and he would triumph.

The cloud of milk-white light that marked the borders of Aquintir's mad world spread broadly to either side of him now—and Jak't'rin reversed his flight, hurtling back up into the darkness. He would not face her on her best ground. Instead he shot into the machine-night, seeking the strands of deeper, corrupting blackness that Aquintir had insinuated there.

He found one, a ribbon of blackness as much an impression as a concrete object, that seemed to coil about a portion of the night it rested against and crush it, contort it into some unhealthy shape it had never been meant to assume. He threw himself on it, wrenching it from its grasp, pinching it off and wrenching at it, until a great length of it tore free and drifted off, to disintegrate an instant later.

At the moment of its breakage, the darkness around Jak't'rin seemed to come alive. Whips and ropes and tendrils of Aquintir-stuff arced in from all directions, lashing at him, flailing around him, seeking to catch him up and crush him into nothingness or twist him into some gross shape that pleased her.

Strands plucked at him, caught corners and folds and pockets of his essence. He clawed free of them, tore them apart, broke them, as fast as they came. But there were always more. . . .

Pain coursed through Aquintir as if hot oil ran in her bones where marrow should have been.

She turned in on herself, worrying at her persona as a sick animal might gnaw at the flesh above some discomfort. She found her tormentor, a mote of uncompromising solidity that burrowed into her, ripping where the machines had sought to ease her loose, tearing where they had merely pried. The agony was beyond description. She pulled her attention away from her world and focussed it on the tormenting mite.

The mountains had stopped.

Anthony Rogers and Ruth Harris slowly eased themselves to a sitting position. They had fallen, finally, their senses overloaded by the heaving earth and the unceasing thunder of the advancing range. Dust filled the air, and coated their faces and hair and clothing. Small patches of red showed where Rogers' cuts had opened again, and there was a bruise on Ruth's jaw that promised to develop spectacularly.

The once-distant mountains looked to be scarcely ten miles off, now. The foothills were a featureless hash of ruined stone.

From somewhere behind them came a keening. Stiffly, they turned, to see Talinai advancing past them toward the broken rock, her fighting stick in her hands. In its way the steady keening that shrilled from her throat was as disquieting as the thunder of the mountains, for it never stopped. She seemed to have no need to draw breath, to stop for a simple inhalation.

She advanced to the nearest boulder, some yards beyond them. The fighting stick rose up above her head and then descended, to strike ringingly against the stone. She struck at the boulder again and again, as chips flew and the metal blades grew twisted and dull. Finally she brought the weapon down with all her strength, and it snapped cleanly halfway up the haft, the ruined warhead flying off into the rubble. Talinai screamed and flung the hilt after it; it clattered away out of sight as she slumped down against the boulder, spent. For all its scars, the stone seemed to have rather more fight left, as rocks will.

"What happened?" Rogers asked. "Why did it stop?"

"I don't know," Ruth said. "Maybe somebody or something changed its mind, or got bored, or thought of something more fun to try. I really don't know. I'm just glad it did."

"Of course, it could start again, anytime."

"Optimist. How's our friend over there?"

"Seems to have quieted down," Rogers answered, studying Talinai. "Want to go check?"

"No thank you. It might decide it wants to hit something else."

"Mm." Rogers looked up at the quiescent mountains. "What do you think we should do now?"

"Well. . . . We won't gain anything by staying here," Ruth said." On the other hand, I'm really reluctant to suggest we head up into those mountains."

"I wonder why," Rogers chuckled. "What about back out onto the plain?"

"Well, there doesn't seem to be anything out there—" Ruth shrugged "—but then again, there doesn't seem to be anything out there. Doesn't seem to be much incentive to take the trouble."

"Except that if we stay here and those mountains start to move again, we're finished," Rogers said.

"True . . . but then you have to figure that if someone who can make mountains walk wants us badly enough, he, she, or it can probably take us."

"True."

"And at least we'd be going somewhere else."

"So, it's off to the mountains, then."

"I guess," Rogers said. He got to his feet. "Come on."

They started toward the rock jumbles. When they reached it, Ruth laid a hand on Rogers' arm and halted him.

"Just a minute, Tony."

She turned to Talinai, slouched against her rock. Ruth pointed to her, then to herself, then up into the mountains. Then they set off again.

"Why'd you do that?" Rogers asked.

"Couldn't hurt. Didn't seem right to just go and leave it sitting there."

"Probably as sensible as what we're doing,"

Rogers said wryly. But when he looked back he could see a small figure climbing up the scree after them.

Talinai watched the creatures climbing away from her. She could not understand it; they had seen what the Monster could do, and yet they insisted on acting, as if anything they could do would matter. More, they seemed to expect her to follow them, as if she hadn't had enough, hadn't learned the pointlessness of further effort. She should let them go, out of her life, gone to where they could bother her anymore. . . .

The plain stretched out before her, vast and empty and lifeless, lonely—

—cursing herself for a fool, she got up and began to climb.

He fought with all his strength, but Jak't'rin could feel himself losing.

For every strand he ripped apart, more came at him. The shredded self-stuff of the strands he had destroyed blended and merged with the new strands coming up against him.

They coiled around him as he tore at them; they bound him, and confined him for all their struggles. And then Aquintir gathered her strength, and bore down on him with all her might.

Jak't'rin cried out as the coiled strands constricted, seeking to rend him as he had rent them. They began to twist, to work, seeking to force openings in his defenses, that they might destroy him.

They failed. As they constricted, Jak't'rin drew himself in, contracting, concentrating himself, to the point where the constructing strands could put no greater pressure on him than he put on himself. As they twisted, he turned with them, and eased the strain, always going with each new attack and robbing it of its strength.

Somewhere, Aquintir screamed in rage, and hurled him out with all her force. Jak't'rin plunged into the white light of the test world, an invisible meteor of identity careening downward above the ruined plains. But he retained control. He could feel Aquintir straining to force him into a conceived identity of her own choice, but she had erred in casting him out of her full strength. Here in the test world she could act on him only indirectly, through the environment she had made her own. Now she was the one constrained by her conceptions; in maintaining his own identity, Jak't'rin had negated much of her strength. But he realized that he could not challenge her directly a second time. He had achieved a standoff. Aquintir could not force her perception of him on him, but in his own identity he lacked the power to impose his on her. She was too strong, too well intertwined with the test system. He would have to find some way of countering her power within the test itself—

—there was a way. He had neutralized a large part of her strength when he had established his own conceived identity firmly; he had denied her that much of the world that she could bend to her will. There was now that much of the test world beyond her control. The key to victory against Aquintir would be to deny her as much of it as possible. She drew her strength from the unity of her mania; shatter that unity and she would shatter. Jak't'rin already knew where he could find three more aspects of the test world not of her creation.

Unformed but coherent, invisible to the light and eyes of Aquintir's world, Jak't'rin sped north, ignoring her imagined gravity and winds, flying swiftly toward the great mountains.

Fear gripped Aquintir as she sought to stay Jak't'rin. She had realized too late that she had given him the means of violating her perceptions. He might still have been an inconsequential, almost microscopic discrepancy, but he was also one she was powerless to correct. He did not merely resist her new attacks upon him, he ignored them, passed them by as though they did not exist, as though she was an ineffectual dream to be ignored. Storm wind and lightning scored him but did no harm; spires of rock and great jets of scalding vapor burst upward from the plain but he passed through them uncaring, driving on toward the mountains.

Suspicion struck her, when she noticed his destination. Two more anomalies already existed, aside from the futile Talinai. She did not believe she wanted them all to meet: one large anomaly might be more trouble than three smaller ones. She abandoned her attacks on Jak't'rin, and turned her attention back to the small figures making their slow way through the mountains' lower slopes.

It had been spectacular, he had to admit that.

For several minutes a solid wall of chaos had erupted out on the plains, a bar-straight line of storm and upheaval that had ravaged a dozen kilometers of land and then vanished as quickly and improbably as it had come. Rogers had been relieved when the line of destruction stopped short of the mountains they ascended, but his relief had been short-lived. No sooner had the disturbances out on the plains died out than the wind began to build around them and the ground began to tremble beneath their feet.

Ruth Harris had turned and looked back at him, face ashen; from somewhere far behind her she faintly heard Talinai's despairing howl. Rogers gestured Ruth ahead, onward, and followed as she scrambled forward.

Daylight fled the mountainside as the sky above them darkened. Thunder rumbled heavily above the wind; the first stones came bounding down from above them.

And the mountains began to shift again.

The movement was too ponderous to allow for any sense of acceleration, but looking down, Rogers could see the narrow valley between the peak they climbed and its neighbor begin to narrow, as the two mountains began to slide toward each other in a froth of displaced soil.

"Hold on!" He shouted, not knowing if Ruth could hear him. He threw himself flat, groping for handholds in the rock as the two mountains collided.

It seemed a gentle enough movement to the small creatures clinging to the vast slope. The mountains struck one another; their bases were crushed and intermingled. Slowly, almost gracefully, the mountains canted toward each other under the impetus of their unguessable momentum. Great fragments of their faces broke loose and slid down into the buried valley; dirt and rock filled the air even as the first bulletlike hailstones struck down.

A shelf of granite fully fifty meters across broke free beneath Talinai, and slid down the heeling slope, bearing her along. The slide was deceptively smooth, its considerable acceleration masked by the size of her platform. She had the absurd notion that if she waited until the shelf was just about to impact at the bottom of the slope and then jumped up, she might be spared the force of the collision. She did not reject the notion, as much as she simply could not be bothered to act on it: it would have required far more of an exertion of will than she was capable of anymore.

The shelf slammed into the intersection between the peaks and its full momentum was suddenly evident. Talinai was torn free of her handholds and rolled and tumbled down the hill in a protective huddle as stone rained down around her. Within seconds she was lost to sight within the clouds of dust and rubble.

Rogers tried to crawl across the heaving slope to where Ruth Harris clung to trembling rock. A bouncing stone struck him heavily in the side, sending him skidding several yards downslope before he could check his fall. He lay still for a moment, fighting for breath that would not come, and then began inching his way back up the mountainside.

Dust stabbed at his eyes and invaded his nostrils. Gravel and small stones pelted him, almost a relief between the stinging impacts of the bullet-size hailstones.

Ruth Harris lay face down, her features obscured by an arm thrown across them protectively or in unconsciousness. Rogers felt a stab of alarm and called out; relief washed through him like adrenalin as she looked up.

He fought his way slowly up the slope. Hail raised egg-sized welts where it struck him— particular stabs of pain indicated a lucky hit on a tender cut. His back was bleeding freely again.

A rock came skidding and tumbling down the hillside. Ruth saw it coming and reached out a warding hand, but it had too much weight on it, too much speed: it knocked her outstretched hand aside and struck Anthony Rogers a stunning blow on the side of the head. His grip slackened reflexively and he slid backward for almost his full progress before he fetched up against a spur of stone. He lay there, dazed, hurting, unable to focus, knowing only that he had to try to get back up the slope, somehow, for some reason—

Jak't'rin hit him like an express train.

There was a sudden mad rush of sensation, a flood of information and half-sensed images and fragments of thought, and then Rogers was resting comfortably inside his own head, comfortably detached from everything, while some harder, fresher persona drove first one hand forward and then another, and started his body back up the slope. . . .

He was back.

He could still feel the presence, flowing around and about his mind—but Anthony Rogers was back in control.

He almost wished he wasn't. There wasn't a single part of his body that didn't hurt, that didn't bear bruise or cut or hailstone welt. They were sheltering in the lee of yet another overhang of rock, three-sided but not quite deep enough to be called a cave. Outside the storm thundered on.

Ruth Harris was staring at him, concern etched on her face—but she was staring at him, and from as far across the recess as she could get.

From somewhere, he dredged up a smile, that stung cracked and swollen lips.

"Hello, Ruth. I think I went away on you for a little while."

"You damned near went away for good, Tony," she said.

"Did I?" he tried to ease himself into a more comfortable position. There wasn't one. "Maybe you'd better tell me about it."

"You stood up." She shuddered. "That rock hit you, and you started to fall, and then that out-cropping caught you—and a moment later, you stood up. You *walked* up that slope; you walked up to me, and the rocks were hitting you and the hailstones, the hailstones were cutting the bandages right off your back. You put yourself between the wind and me, and you helped me to my feet—and you *looked* at me." She couldn't meet his eyes again. "I've never seen an expression like that in my life, Tony. I hope to God I never see it again. You looked like you could have ordered that mountain to stand still by yourself."

"No, I couldn't have done that, Ruth."

"Anyway, you started walking forward again, and I followed you. I don't know how long we walked, but finally you reached this place, and you stopped—and you just fell, Tony, as if you'd just realized how badly you'd been beaten. I wish I knew how you did that. I wish I knew what happened to you."

"I'm all right, Ruth."

"And I wish I could believe that."

"I'm fine," he assured her again, trying to

make sense out of what was going on inside his head. "Something did happen to me out there; I don't know what. But I'm fine." He felt the tiredness coming over him again. "At least in my head."

If she made any reply, he was asleep before he heard it.

It was as if his eyes awoke her.

Ruth Harris jerked upright as she saw his expression.

"Tony?" He continued to stare at her. "Tony, what is it?"

Take a hawk, a peregrine, a plunging killer, from its skies. Transfer its mind, its soul, the essence of its carnivorous nature, to the mind of a man. You would get such an expression as Ruth Harris saw.

"Ruth." The word came out flat, short. "We cannot stay here."

"What?"

"We must move on."

"In that?" Outside, the storm raged on with undiminished fury.

"The storm is no longer a concern."

"You're kidding. Tony, what's the matter with you?"

Rogers was on his feet and moving out of the overhang. The storm blew and raged around him—and left him untouched. No hailstone rebounded from abused flesh; the leaping, falling rocks missed him cleanly, every time. When he

had stood there long enough to prove that it was
no fluke, he stepped back into the niche.

"I've . . . been learning things," he said. His
expression altered. Something softer, something—human—entered it. "I can beat the storm
now, and I think I can protect you, too. Come
on."

"No. I'm not moving until you tell me what's
going on here."

Rogers took a step toward her. Without thinking, she reached for her pistol. He stopped.

"Is it that bad?" he said. He sighed. "All right.
I'll explain. But I'll explain while we walk."

Ruth Harris looked at him with something
very close to horror in her eyes.

"Can you get him out again?" she asked.

"No," Rogers said. "No, I don't think so.
Jak't'rin was only able to merge with me because
we're both 'anomalies,' as he calls us, in Aquintir's world. I don't think he quite understood
what he was doing, though. In any real sense, we
don't exist here, physically. When Jak't'rin
merged with me, he merged the concepts of Anthony Rogers and himself. I'm not sure it's possible to separate them again—and I'm not sure he
wants to."

"But what does that do to Tony Rogers?"

"Nothing. Everything." He turned to face her,
calm and quiet in the storm that raged all around
them but left them somehow untouched,
through Jak't'rin's strength. "I'm still Anthony

Rogers," he said. "Everything that made me what I am is still there, still complete—only now there's more. And there may be more yet," he finished quietly. "But Tony Rogers won't ever go away."

"What's it like?" she asked. "To have a Prl'lu inside your head?"

"Impressive," he said, slowly. "There's a—surety, a self-confidence about them that's hard to explain. It's even kind of hard to believe."

"But doesn't he know he's your enemy?"

"We've all got an enemy now: Aquintir. That's his one priority. After that—he has plans, and so do I. It could be interesting."

"Where are we going now?"

"Wherever Aquintir wants us."

"What the hell is the point of that?" Ruth Harris asked.

"It will draw her out against us. The purpose now is to show her that her efforts against us through the storm are failing."

"And then what do we do?"

"Fight her."

"Oh. Right."

They moved on along the mountainside, as the storm swirled impotently around them.

I'm glad I made it sound so simple, Rogers thought. *'It's nothing serious, just an alien intelligence shacking up inside my head.'* It was indeed, an 'impressive' experience, to be able to turn around within one's own mind and look out over an enormous vista of memory that had never been there before, a vista that pulsed with images and feelings as yet indecipherable. He might have resented it, had he not known that Jak't'rin was as unsettled by their merger as he was. The Prl'lu honestly seemed to have felt that their joining was to have been a temporary phenomenon—he had never expected the seeming permanency of the bond.

Oddly, it was not as though there were two people suddenly in his mind. Instead it felt to Rogers as though he had suddenly attained an entire new level of memory and knowledge, as though years of life had suddenly come awake with all the suddenness of a switched-on light-bulb. He wondered if it felt the same for Jak't'rin, if Jak't'rin still existed as such, and if so, whether Jak't'rin felt the same pity for him. . . .

Jak't'rin was more impressed than he had thought he would be. He had felt brief alarm at having merged with a being that considered itself an enemy of his people, but studies of his new memory showed that the being had more than ample reason. It no longer worried Jak't'rin; if his strategy succeeded, there would be no further prospect of combat, and Prl'lu knew only to defeat their opponents, not to hate them.

The 'human' mind itself was a fascinating thing, he discovered. Nothing like as effective in a straight-line way as his own mental processes, but certainly complex and fairly capable over a broader range of functions, if that was held desirable. And for all its alien differences, there were a great number of congruencies between the human mind and Jak't'rin's own—the human seemed as firmly committed to preserving its own people as Jak't'rin was to his, and it seemed almost as single-minded about it. There was a refreshing, almost Blood-like quality to Rogers' continued defiance of his race's destiny.

Jak't'rin decided he had chosen himself a good tool.

Her rage howled and battered at the two figures marching across her mountains, to no avail. Storm ripped and slashed at them, with no effect. The mountainsides crumbled and flowed like breaking waves, but never atop them. It was as if they refused to notice her attacks. Aquintir would not accept it; she could not. Such defiance warped the very fabric of her mad reality in ways it could never survive. She gathered up all her strength and flung herself down into her world, to do final battle for her soul.

Talinai lay where the stones had thrown her.

The scree itself made a passable windbreak, and as she watched the chaos on the mountainsides she knew she could go no further. Let the testers make of that what they would; she had had enough, and more than anyone could expect her to take.

No more stone cascaded down atop her; even

the storm seemed less fierce around her. No
doubt the Monster's attention was elsewhere.
The thought of the mad Aquintir triumphant
only increased her weariness. Any sense of responsibility she might have felt for a world she
no longer believed she would see again was long
burnt out of her.

The howling began again, but she paid it no
attention. It could not concern her this time, she
had yielded, the Monster must know that. It was
not worth her while to come at her again.

She was almost right. Only one of the bounding nightmares that swarmed around her into the
mountains paused long enough to kill her.

In the outside world, a crystalline tube glowed
blue for an instant. When the cerulean glow vanished, the tube was empty.

Jak't'rin felt Talinai's death, of course. There
was nothing in the test world that could possibly
be beyond his knowledge, the machines had
seen to that. For a moment he regretted not having saved her, a vestige of his fleshly Prl'lu heritage, but it passed. The purpose of the test was to
determine the strongest of the Shapers, the ones
most fit to rule. With any luck, it would still do
that.

The storm was dying around them, and they
could both—the three of them?—hear the howling in the distance.

"What are those things?" Ruth asked.

"Aquintir," Rogers told her, as the knowledge came clear in his own mind. "Or as much of her as she can intrude directly on this level. She's coming to finish this now."

"Will she?"

"One way or another," Rogers agreed.

"Right," Ruth said calmly enough, though the breath was thin beneath her voice. She drew her pistol and looked around. "The cover's pretty good up there. I hope this thing still remembers how to shoot."

"No," Rogers said. He pointed down between the mountains, to where the tortured valley widened into a vale almost a kilometer across. "We'll go down there. We'll need the space."

"For what?"

"To fight her."

"In the middle of an open field? And just how do you propose to do that?" Ruth asked.

"Successfully, I hope." For a moment, his grin was unadulterated Anthony Rogers. "Come on."

They boiled out of the canyon in a dark wave, a mass of murderous sublife that roiled forward like a flood, the color of befouled water.

Two figures faced them, all but lost in the middle of the open field. Ruth Harris had her pistol, Anthony Rogers the accumulated knowledge of the Prl'lu and the Prl'arek machines. It would have to be enough.

"Do you know what you're seeing now?" he said. "That's Aquintir, all of her that we'll probably ever see. Not a pretty sight, is it?"

"What can she *be*, Tony, to create something like that?"

"Nothing much different from us in kind, only in degree. That's the part of her that's twisted this world, that perverted the test and murdered the Shapers she competed against. If we can beat that, we've got the key to defeating her."

"We have to beat all that by ourselves. . . ."

"Not at all. We won't be alone in this."

That is an actual part of Aquintir, his memories told him, created by and of her. To defeat her we must reply in kind, match creation with creation.

The field around them grew populous.

Ruth Harris cried out as the angular Prl'lu warrior seemed to materialize out of the very earth beside her, armed with javelin, spear and stick, cousin to the dozens and hundreds of others spreading out across the field.

Rogers looked at the assembled warriors with amusement. "I don't think all the parties involved have been heard from yet," he said.

The field to the other side him of turned khaki. They stood ranked there as he had last seen them, pie-plate helmets dented and scarred, uniforms grimy with weapons-smoke and dust, just as they had been on the day they came marching back out of the wheat, pounded and scarred but unbeaten, the long bayonets gleaming in the bright summer sun. Others stood beyond the ranked marines, as he remembered them—

Cockney riflemen with their square, heavy Lee-Enfields, faceless poilus drawn up in rank after rank. Here and there the boxlike silhouette of an ancient tank rose up between blocks of infantry; high overhead came a droning as of enormous bees.

Ruth looked from their sudden host out toward their attackers. Had that turbulent mob actually hesitated, at the sight of this fresh opposition, or was it merely a lull in their chaotic progress.

Whatever it had been, it was over. With a shriek from uncounted throats Aquintir's hordes leaped forward to close with their foes and do murder.

The world twisted under her as Aquintir's enemies summoned their might. The sudden presence of so much power not under her control cut her like a knife, but she did not yield to it. It had become a question of survival now, but in her maddened state she had never considered it anything else. There was room in her vision for no will but hers, and she meant to keep it so. . . .

A thousand guns rippled with flame. The left flank of Aquintir's host became even more chaotic as bodies were pierced and fell, bringing their followers down atop them. The droning in the sky increased to a roar as the Bristols and the De Havilands plummeted down out of the sky to

loose their bombs into the massed horror beneath them, and the Spads and Nieuports
skimmed low over the nightmares, Vickers and
Lewis guns chattering. Carnage was wrought
among Aquintir's creatures; they died by the
hundreds.

But they had those hundreds to spare, and
thousands more. They kept coming.

There was a clattering of hooves from behind
the human troops and their ranks parted, to let
batteries of wooden-wheeled, horse-drawn
seventy-fives pass forward. The crews swiftly
unlimbered their fieldpieces and set to work,
pumping shell after shell into the horde. High
explosive tore deep into their ranks; case shot
flayed the foremost.

The swarm had come within range now. As
rifles and cannon snapped and thundered a hail
of javelins rose into the air, sleeting down amidst
them as the Prl'lu came into the battle. A wave of
throwing spears followed, and a second. More of
Aquintir's creatures died, pierced by barbed
shaft or leaden pellet. But they kept coming.

With a roar of defiance as loud as anything
their enemies had uttered the Prl'lu host charged
forward to meet them, and the ranks of human
troops born of Rogers' memory ran alongside
them. Long, keen bayonets were levelled ahead
of marine and tommy; mounted cavalry in
broad-brimmed campaign hats at last made the
long charge that Hiram Maxim's invention had
denied them five hundred years ago, brandishing sabers and Colt pistols.

The two bodies met in a thunderous collision,

and Aquintir's host was stopped where it stood. Clawed horrors gibbered and slashed at khaki fabric and bleeding flesh. Clubbed Springfields and bayonets bludgeoned and thrust deeply. Fighting stick and buckler challenged fang and claw.

The planes came low again, sweeping over the battle, machine guns chattering. The tanks drove deep into the ranks of their enemies, crushing and killing even as Aquintir's minions swarmed over them. Men died, Prl'lu died, monsters died.

It seemed to go on for hours.

The troops poured past Rogers and Harris in an unbroken swarm. The horrors poured down out of the hills without end.

Ruth had made heavy use of her weapon in the early part of the battle, firing rocket after rocket in support of the artillery. She had stopped long since; it was making no discernible difference.

"How long can this go on?" she shouted above the distant roaring. The chaos of battle had become the sort of overwhelming, ongoing drone one heard near a great waterfall.

"Until Aquintir is exhausted, or we are."

"There ought to be a more definite way of deciding this."

"There isn't. It's a question of winning or losing—" Rogers broke off. An expression that might have been delight lit up his face. "Ruth, have I ever told you that you are one very smart lady?"

"I haven't felt like one lately. What are you talking about?"

"There *is* a way. But Jak't'rin can't see it. He

doesn't know where to look. He's a Prl'lu and he can't see beyond fighting an enemy to how to beat it."

"What are you going to do?"

"What Jak't'rin did to me." He looked out at the milling warriors. "You'd better move back, Ruth. Quite a ways."

Ruth looked at him, and backed away.

"Farther."

She was a good fifty meters away from him when the change began.

Rogers knew what Jak't'rin thought of him; how could he not? And this was the time when the 'complexity' of his human mind would serve their cause better than Jak't'rin's linear, protective conditioning.

He had told Ruth Harris that they faced the darkest part of Aquintir, that aspect of her that had distorted and perverted the test. Fine then. He would fight blackness with blackness.

He dug into his mind, deeply, into the parts and places where few people could look, where even he could manipulate but not observe too closely. He fastened a great bundle of self-stuff, brought it forth, and cast it out.

A shadow began to form around Anthony Rogers where he stood, a shadow that took on the shape of a man many times greater than man-size—but a twisted manshape, hunchbacked and long-armed, shambling and evocative of fright-ened childhood nights. It towered up above him, and even from where she stood Ruth Harris could perceive the smell of it, a smell of sweat and soiled bodies and decay.

The shadow turned from Rogers, and shambled toward the battle. It brushed through the lesser dream-warriors without noticing, deep into Aquintir's host—

—and it began to feed.

Where it trod upon Aquintir's nightmares they vanished before it raised its foot again. When they struck at it they were caught, and held fast, and drawn into its midnight bulk. It reached down and caught up squirming horrors in writhing handsful, and crammed them into its face, where they vanished. The obscenities around it gibbered and capered and fought and tried to flee, but there was no fleeing. The shadow overstrode them all, and drew them in.

Aquintir at last knew true horror, as she felt great parts of herself being leached away. This was not the slow diffusion she had felt as she fought the machines; this was dismemberment, this was violent amputation of her self. She threw aside all thoughts of fighting and withdrew, pulled herself free—

—and was stopped, by a thread of shadow running back into the light of the world, a thread extruded from her self and bound inextricably to the world she had created, and which now fatally defined her. . . .

The shadow lumbered back to where Rogers stood, trailing its thread of darkness like the string of a child's balloon. It paused before him, and looked down with its eyeless face.

Rogers looked up at it, hesitating. He had known—he had thought he had known—what he was doing when he summoned up the shadow and cast it forth, and he had not thought he labored under any delusions as to his own inner purity—but to actually see such blackness made manifest before him, and to have to take it back—he couldn't, he—

—he had to. Unless he took the shadow back into himself it would be as if he had done nothing against Aquintir; he would have traded off one blackness for another. He couldn't do that; he couldn't allow it. This was his responsibility.

He reached out a hand and touched the tree-trunk-thick leg before him, and the shadow began to fade, to shrink, dwindling down as he took its essence back into himself, until he was left alone, holding the black thread of Aquintir's self that it had brought him.

Ruth Harris approached him slowly.

"Tony?" He looked up at her; he seemed to have aged ten years in as many seconds. "Is it over?"

"Very nearly. This is the end of it, I think." And he focussed his attention on the thread in his hand and began to draw it in. . . .

Four of the crystalline tubes at the end the great chamber were still occupied. Two of them slid open.

Rogers and Harris stepped down, and faced the metal guardian.

"The system has been restored," he said—but he spoke in the rolling tongue of the Prl'arek, drawing on knowledge from the others within him. "Further corporal maintenance is no longer justified."

"Acknowledged. Request clarification of final system distortion."

"Final—oh, yes." He turned and looked down the chamber, to where mad Couilin rested in his cylinder. Final system distortion is irreparable. Purge system on external authority."

"Acknowledged." Three tubes glowed briefly with blue light. *"Purge completed."*

"Very well. Open the chamber. The system is released from active state." Rogers and Harris turned and walked away toward the ramp entrance. The stasis shield dropped away as they passed through it and climbed upward.

"Will this work, Tony?"

"It should," he said, "I know enough, now. It will have to. We need this world, if we're ever going to get ours back."

Part of him complained that he should not have to 'get' his world back, that the two worlds were his now, he had passed the test, fulfilled his responsibility. But that part of him was not human, and did not understand that to return to Earth and enforce his authority, he would have to stay alive long enough to make it clear once he got there.

They left the ramp at the vehicle level. Daylight flooded in through the shattered doors, the pierced walls.

They reached the front of the chamber, and began to pass the machines that had been damaged in battle. *That was unfortunate*, Rogers thought, *we'll need those.*

He paused beneath the ruined gate, before turning to look outside.

"Ruth," he said, "do you understand what's happened to me, what we've been through down there?"

"I'd be lying if I said that I did—or that I liked it."

Rogers nodded. "And how do you feel about me, about what I've become?" He looked at her. "I can't change it, now. It's too late for that and in any case I'll need everything I've learned, if I'm to pull this off. This is probably the last chance I'll have to ask you."

"I've seen a lot of things happen to you that scared the hell out of me, Tony—but you say you're still Tony Rogers, and as far as I'm concerned, your asking this proves it. I think I'll take a chance on you yet."

He grinned. "That's a victory right there." He looked out at the field. "All right. Let's get this started."

"*Captain Jefferson!*" Peggy Biskani called. "Look back at the gates!"

Jefferson swung his turret quickly to bring his

screen to bear, alarmed at the urgency in her voice.

"It's Doctor Harris—and the *Marshal!*"

It was. They came out of the ruined gateway, walking toward the fighting machine as though out for a lazy summer's stroll, unconcerned and not needing to be about their surroundings.

"Cover the treeline," Jefferson ordered. "If you see anything moving, open up on it."

They were level with the vehicle now. Jefferson heard the distant clang as Biskani threw a hatch open, heard her call to them—

—and watched as Rogers walked right by the vehicle. Ruth Harris disappeared from view— presumably she was being sensible and boarding the vehicle.

Peggy Biskani's voice reached him through his earphones.

"Captain, Doctor Harris says we're to hold our fire, whatever happens next."

"Dammit, Peg, those woods are full of Prl'lu!"

"She says those are the Marshal's orders, Captain."

"What the hell is going on? All right, all hands, you heard the word. Do not fire, repeat do not fire under any circumstances."

Unless Rogers dies out there, he amended silently. *Whereupon we are going to put this thing in gear and sterilize this mudball.*

Rogers paused, fifty meters outside the treeline, well within javelin cast.

"*Ahgn'ki Prl'lu,*" he called. Did something

move out there? He couldn't be sure.

There was no further response.

Words alone won't do it, he thought. *You knew that. You'll have to go whole hog.*

He reached down, deep into his knowledge of Shaper and Blood, and found what he sought. He put forth his will seeking, touching the hidden warriors one after another, awakening the obedience that had waited there for generations.

"*Ahgn'ki Prl'lu,*" he called again.

And this time they came.

They filtered forward from the trees; they stood upright from hiding places in the tall grass that the men and women in the fighting machine had never seen dug. And they came forward, to cluster around him, seeking to understand this strange being who could so compel them. Rogers sighed, and began the process that would with any luck let humanity strike peace with the Prl'lu. The harsh, glottal words irritated his throat. He wished he'd learned a magic trick that could soften syllables. The future seemed to belong to the hoarse. . . .

Slowly, Aquintir took stock of her new surroundings. It wasn't the best mind she could have hoped for, but it seemed infinitely preferable to the oblivion she had been sure was her fate when Rogers had consumed her. But he could not have destroyed her, and could not destroy her now, she saw that. He needed her knowledge, her skills—and that made him vulnerable.

She began to reach out, seeking the limits of the consciousness surrounding her, looking to insinuate herself as she had before—

—and Jak't'rin was there, solid and implacable, blocking her off.

You will not do that, she heard. *You are strong, yes, but you are twisted, wrong. The human is a lesser power than you but he is an honest steward, and I will honor that stewardship. If you seek to pervert him, I will oppose you—and I will not lose.*

With a soundless cry of rage Aquintir launched herself upon the Prl'lu defender, in the first attack of a battle that would never end. . . .

ANDRE NORTON

Witch World Series

Enter the Witch World for a feast of adventure and enchantment, magic and sorcery.

FRITZ LEIBER

FAFHRD AND THE GRAY MOUSER SAGA